The Eighth Day

J. Boss

authorHOUSE®

AuthorHouse™
1663 Liberty Drive, Suite 200
Bloomington, IN 47403
www.authorhouse.com
Phone: 1-800-839-8640

First published by AuthorHouse 8/26/2008

ISBN: 978-1-4259-7198-4 (sc)

Printed in the United States of America
Bloomington, Indiana

This book is printed on acid-free paper.

To Jimmy and Diane who allowed me life.
Thanks!

To JeMarion and Jayden who have made it worth living.
Mommy loves you.

To Dee who helped me figure out where all this was leading to.
Thanks for helping me cry my way there. You're the best counselor
money can't buy. There will never be another you.

Last, but not least, to every 'Jacob' in my life
(and there have been many)
You pushed me to another level. I wouldn't have had it any
other way.
I pray nothing but blessings upon you all!

Preface

Believe it or not, when I started writing this book, it was never supposed to be published. It was a form of therapy to get me through a very difficult time in my life. I had just gotten out of a failed relationship and was severely depressed. I'm the type of woman that gives my all when I'm in love with a man. The flip side of that is that once he's gone, there's not very much of me left to pick up the pieces. I normally like to think that I'm the type who lives life without regrets. This time, however, I felt like a chunk of me was missing that I didn't know how to get back. Most days I didn't even want to get out of bed. One day I just got tired of feeling that way. I sat at my computer and began to type frantically. The more I wrote the better I felt. I actually finished chapters 1-3 in one sitting. I tried to just write and not read what I was putting on paper, but I couldn't help going back over things. One day it hit me that I actually liked reading what I had written. I sent it to a few friends to get their input, and they loved it. They began to tell others, and before long I had people waiting in line to see what the ending would be. Still, I had no plans of publishing the story. I mean just because your mother likes your art project doesn't mean you're the next Van Gogh. It seemed, though, that the more people I allowed read in part, the more I had people approaching me wanting to read the whole story. I finally decided to test the waters with complete strangers. I met several people at the salon that I frequented and just asked them to read the first chapter or so. There was an overwhelming demand for me to finish the book and get copies in circulation. I was flattered, but still not convinced.

What really did it for me was when a woman asked me if this was a true story about me. While I have taken some very loose examples of my personal experiences and woven them into the story, this is by no means an autobiography. She seemed so disappointed when I told her it wasn't a book about my life. She said that she had been through something similar to what was described in the book and that she could really relate to Shamonica. I knew exactly what she meant. I also felt like Shamonica was a friend of mine. She was someone I knew. Her experience was not so different from my own. I couldn't wait to see how things turned out for her. If Shamonica could make it, then maybe there was an inkling hope for me. I thought I was feeling that way because I was writing the story. Then I realized that I was making others feel that way by allowing them to read it.

I have worked in the medical field for over eight years. My job is extremely rewarding. Every day, I love to see the lives that I touch. This, however, is a different kind of reward. I may not be saving lives by making this book available to you, but I may actually be saving hope for someone. I wanted to publish this so that every woman (or man) who has ever had a "Jacob experience" (or "Jackie experience") could have someone to relate to. I don't profess to have any answers to the many questions about why people do what they do in relationships. God knows I'm not the authority on what makes relationships work. What I can do is give people something real to read about and hopefully make them think while entertaining the public in the process.

My disclaimer to any Jacob (or Jackie) who may be reading this is that this book was not made to bash you. Maybe you can be made to think about the choices you make that may drastically affect the lives of those who love you…whether you love them or not.

j.b.

Chapter One
The Breakup

"Girl, I told you about fuckin' with them damned Africans. They're crazy as hell!"

Lena was right. She had told me a million times about "them damned Africans" especially one in particular. I let her rattle off her million-and-one-reasons-to-forget- about-him speech as I slipped in and out of consciousness. I was only half listening, but that was okay. She was only half talking. She had given this oration so many times that she could probably recite it in her sleep. My bedroom became a courtroom, and Lena was the judge and jury. The verdict was always the same when it came to Jacob: guilty. She rattled off all the reasons he had been wrong for me from day one. She insisted on telling me how blessed I was that he was now out of my life. I listened and tried to act as if I cared. Meanwhile, I was attempting to figure out how I could've allowed myself to get where I was that day. Jacob and I had been together for almost five years. We had been raising a child together for four years, living together for two, and today he had married another woman. Just like that! Nine days before our five-year anniversary. He had dismissed me like I was nothing.

There were no kind words that were going to ease this. I suppose that's why Lena didn't offer any. Instead, she just wrapped her arms around me and let me lay there, pitiful and helpless, until I cried myself to sleep. The Xanax she had given me did more good than any words ever could. Lena was my big sister and one of my closest friends. She had never trusted Jacob from the beginning. I suppose it's just my nature to trust people. I mean he seemed like the perfect man for me right from the start. He always opened doors for me. He never forgot a birthday or holiday. He was great with my son Mathieu. He was always willing to attend any event I scheduled or said I enjoyed. The slick bastard even had my mama in love with him! The one flaw he had was that he was a liar. Not just any kind of liar, oh no, not my Jacob! He could sell salt to a slug and convince him it was skin conditioner. This man was smooth. He was everything a woman would want, and nothing any woman needs. He was tall with dark skin that was smooth enough to make you want to stand eye to eye with him just to see if he was real or one of those plastic manikins. He had a bald head that would shine in just the right spot when he laughed. I swear sometimes when he looked at me with those deep, dark eyes I thought he could see straight through me. It was like he always knew what I was thinking or was going say next. He would look at me with those intriguing eyes and suck me right in with his Nigerian accent. He had me wide open right from the day we met.

Lena had thrown a patio party five years ago with her friend Naji, and that was where we first saw one another. Lena was a nurse at the time. Naji was a nurse extern about to graduate college. Naji was a tall, dark-skinned Nigerian sister with just enough beauty to make a man desire to have her, and just enough attitude to let him know when to step off. It was no surprise that she would have a brother as gorgeous as Jacob. Naji never talked much about her family. All I knew was that her mother was still in Nigeria and wanted to come to the states to visit after Naji finished school. Naji even mentioned that she was trying to get her mother to agree to live here since her father had passed away several years prior. She never mentioned a brother. I would've remembered. There would have been no way to forget this man.

He strolled into the party just like any other guest, but there was just something different about him. He had a friend with him who was a bit shorter and not as attractive. It was warm out, but there was a nice breeze blowing. I remember thinkin' to myself, "Lord, just blow that man my way!" He had on a nice blue button down shirt with a pair of nicely starched blue jeans. You would've thought it was a tailored three-piece suit the way the women were all eyeing him. I kept busy the entire night sipping my drink and mostly pretending not to notice him. He caught me looking one too many times.

"You could say 'hello' or something," he teased with that sexy accent of his.

"I thought you American women were more hospitable."

"Wherever would you get an idea like that?" I smiled coyly.

"Well, my sister tells me that there are plenty of nice American women where she works and also at her school. I figured you might be one of them since you are here."

"And who is your sister?" I asked, still dumbfounded that I was even holding a conversation with this perfect creature.

"Nilaja is my sister. This is her party. Or didn't you know that?" he smiled.

Even then the bastard had a smart mouth and was a little too smug. It's amazing the things in life a cute face and a big dick can make up for. He had called Naji by her real name, though, so I knew he must've been telling the truth. Very few people even knew her real name. Nilaja didn't seem so difficult to me, but she said she got tired of everyone in the U.S. mispronouncing it. She asked us to just call her Naji.

"Well, actually, this is also *my* sister's party. Lena and Naji decided to throw this together. Didn't *you* know *that*?"

"Look, lady, I really think you're pretty. I've been noticing you all night. I know you have been noticing me as well. Why don't we just dance so we can get a closer look at one another?"

"I don't even know your name." I mumbled as I tried and failed miserably to act uninterested.

"My name is Jacob," he said as he grabbed my hand and kissed it.

And with that, he whisked me into his arms. I remember thinking to myself how soft his lips were against my hand. I couldn't wait to feel them pressed against mine. He probably read that, too, because he made me wait. We danced and talked all night. Naji and Lena didn't even notice us until the party was almost over. Lena couldn't hide the look of displeasure on her face. She wasn't trying to, but even if she had been, it was there. Naji just smiled nicely and said, "Oh, I see you have met my brother."

"Yes" I smiled, "I guess you could say I have."

Lena and I argued all the way home about how

she didn't want me seeing him and how she could just tell by looking at him that he was all wrong for me. I reminded her that I was a grown ass woman and would do as I damn well pleased. That was just what I did. Six weeks later we were dating exclusively. Six months after that Jacob and I found out I was eight weeks pregnant with Jackson. I didn't plan for it to happen that way, but I wasn't disappointed, either. Jacob and I had already discussed how each of us felt about having children and I knew how he felt about me. I already had a three-year old child who Jacob interacted with very well. I didn't think it would be a bad idea for Mathieu to have a sibling. We decided to have the baby.

Jacob was wonderful during my pregnancy. He rubbed my feet, my back, and anything else I said felt like it needed rubbing. He was always willing to cater to my cravings. Sometimes that meant getting out of bed in the middle of the night to find my favorite junk food, but Jacob never complained. He never got upset with me when I was having one of my mood swings. Everything was outstanding when I was pregnant, especially the sex. As far as I was concerned, Jacob was perfect from his sexy bald head right down to his feet which he kept groomed with regular pedicures. Even his dick was perfect! Not one of the ones with a crook in it. Mr. Cole (the love pole) was just the right shape, color, and width to make a woman want to see what he tasted like without even being prompted. When we made love, I didn't know whether to grab the headboard and run, or stay where I was so he could make me squeal with delight as he plunged into the depth of my soul. I guess that's why it was so easy for me to believe Jacob when he told me I was the one for him. "Baby," he said, "you are the woman God created for me!" I fell for that lame mess, too. Hook, line, and sinker! Now here I was five years later with no ring, two kids, and a hole in my heart big enough to drain all the life out of me with just one more beat.

He had called me at work six days prior and said we needed to talk. He dropped the boys off at my mother's house and made reservations at our favorite spot. He said not to worry about getting dressed up. He just wanted to see me right away. I just knew this was the big moment I had been waiting for. He was finally going to ask me to marry him. I had already been his wife. Cooking and cleaning were not chores to me. They had become a way of life. I loved doing it, too. As corny as it sounds, it was like labor of love. Not only that, but I had stood by him through a lot of drama. I had helped him get his criminal charges thrown out of court for an assault that he had been charged with before we met. He, of course, assured me he didn't do it. He said that some girl he had tried to cut loose got her feelings hurt, and the only way to get back at him was to trump up these fake charges. I had a cousin who had been through something similar in the past, so I asked him to help Jacob out. I cleared his debt with the IRS when a business deal went bad and his partner left him holding the bag. All it took was a little persuading of the auditor. My daddy always said I had the gift of gab. I'm sure those fake receipts I came up with didn't hurt either. I even helped him pay off that raggedy ass truck of his! I had worked the hell out of the title! Now I wanted my just due.

We met at one of my favorite restaurants downtown. Jacob always knew how to woo me. This was the same restaurant we had come to on our first date. I still remember how nervous I was that night. I was thinking to myself how lucky I was to be with him then. Every eye in the room seemed to acknowledge his entrance. All the single women, and some of the attached ones, eyed him down to see what occasion had called this god-like presence from the heavens. Men grabbed the hands of their significant others as if to protect them. It was no use. I swear I think I saw one woman swoon as he passed her table. Jacob never let his eyes fully scan the room. He kept his eyes on me as he made his way to my table. I stood up, he kissed my hand, and just like that he had me. Without even so much as a 'hello' or 'good evening' the man had stolen my heart. We talked for hours that night. He told me he was an auto mechanic and that he was trying to save up enough money to buy his own shop. I told him about my job at the advertising agency and my odd jobs on the side. He seemed very interested in the fact that I was a single mother and that I had plans to work my way up to partner or branch off and start my own company. He said he liked my ambition. All that was years away, though. We both were just focusing on that evening. I'm convinced that it was that night that I fell in love with Jacob. Our first kiss was outside on the restaurant patio. The jazz band was playing in the background. As his full, soft lips grazed across mine I began to feel like I was floating. All else around me disappeared. He pressed his body against mine and I became intoxicated by his scent. I felt like the luckiest woman alive.

The Bass Line was a nice little quiet spot. We would sometimes go there just for the live jazz. Back then, I used to feel like no one could ever love me like Jacob. He would take me anywhere I wanted to go. I knew he couldn't afford some of the places we went, but he hung in there anyway. I remember thinking to myself how in love he must've been with me to spend his last few dollars just to have a few moments of my time. He never acted like it was a big deal. As a matter of fact, he would suggest places to me based on what he thought I liked. He was never wrong. That was my Jacob. He could always read people. He could see a person's innermost thoughts and feelings just by asking a question or two. I liked that! It had been a long time since I felt comfortable being myself around a man. Our conversations were about everything from sports to politics to the freaky things we planned to do later in the evening. We were so happy in those early days.

Now here we were sitting across from each other with him looking at me like he was about to burst open with whatever he had to tell me. He had on a new suit that I had picked out for him just this Christmas. He smelled good, too. I had gotten him some cologne from a little boutique around the corner from my job. I knew the girl who owned the place, and she gave me a sample of one of her new fragrances before it even hit the shelves. I could tell he had something serious on his mind because he kept fidgeting with his napkin. I thought it was cute! This tall, statuesque sculpture of perfection was actually nervous to talk to *me* about something. It had to be huge. Tonight was my big night.

"Shamonica" *Wow, my whole name!* Now I knew it was something big. There was something uneasy in his tone, but I thought he was just nervous.

"Yeah, baby. What's on your mind?"

"How long have we been together now? Like 4...5 years?"

"It'll be five years on the 24th of this month, Jacob." I knew he was just testing me. He never forgot dates.

"Riiight. And in all that time, have I ever given you reason to believe that I would do anything to intentionally hurt you?"

"No, baby. Why do you ask? You're startin' to make me nervous."

"Look, 'Mo,'" *So now I'm 'Mo' again? What the...* "Baby, this is really hard for me to say to you –"

"Well, just spit it out, then, Jacob." I felt the angry little black woman that I tried to keep quiet most of the time rising up in me as I raised my right eyebrow. I was trying to convince her that now was not the time to show up, even though I felt like I needed her to be on standby.

"Mo, I'm having a baby with someone and we've decided to get married."

I felt all the blood that used to be in my head sink to my stomach. All at once, I felt dizzy and nauseated. A red veil dropped down over the room and nobody was there but Jacob and me. I remember thinking to myself that it was better that way. There would be no witnesses to the murder the angry little black woman was about to commit. The words 'baby' and 'married' rang over and over in my head, but they didn't sound right not being associated with me.

Where has he been hiding this other woman? Who the hell is she? What does he mean by 'we decided'? How long has he been keeping this from me? As my head began to pound and vibrate with thoughts and questions, he kept talking.

"Now I know that this may be hard for you to understand, but this is the way things are. You'll just have to deal with it. I have already removed my name and my part of the money from the bank account."

'*The* bank account'? Did he mean the account that *he* suggested *we* open so that it would be easier for *us* to pay bills? *Together*?

"My brother is at the house right now getting my things, so I won't be coming back to the house tonight."

His things? From *the* house? Was this the same house that we called *our* home?

"I'll be by this weekend to take Jackson to his game. Please have him ready early. I plan to take him by to see my mother before we go to the game."

Was he referring to the same mother that I had helped obtain citizenship into this country? The same mother whom I accepted into my home even though I didn't feel she gave me anywhere near the respect I deserved?

"I have already talked to my lawyer about making arrangements with you for child support. Someone will be contacting you tomorrow with the details."

And just like that, Jacob Owodunni walked out of my life. I don't remember too much after that. Just that damned Heather Headly song on the radio when I pulled up in my driveway. The two-car garage was empty. I pulled up on my side of it. As the garage door closed behind me I just sat there staring into the empty space where Jacob would not be parking that night.

In my miiiind I'll always be his lady…and in my miiind I'll always be his girl.

As Heather continued to belt out her tune, I turned off the engine and prepared myself to walk into the emptiness that was now my home.

Chapter Two
Game Day

It was Saturday. Just four days since Jacob had broken the news to me. I had not been able to think about anything else. All I could hear was 'baby' and 'married' over and over. I went to work and sat there for eight hours a day staring at my office door. It was like I was waiting for someone to come through it to give me the answers I needed. Jacob and I stopped talking on Thursday. I didn't see the point of calling him anymore since all I got were lies. He refused to tell me how long the affair had been going on or even the identity of the woman he chosen over his family. Any conversations we had were counter-productive. He was dead set on the fact that I would just have to 'deal with it'. So deal with it I did. Somehow I managed to get up enough strength to get Jackson ready for his game on Saturday. He had been looking forward to it all week, and I didn't want him to be disappointed.

He was one of the best players on the peewee soccer team. I would've taken him myself had I not had to work. I didn't really feel like working either, but I had to finish this project. I found it almost impossible to focus at the office this week. This was my first day alone, and my last chance to make up for all my slacking. Mathieu was at my myother's, Jackson had his game, and I was determined not to let this thing with Jacob get the best of me. I had been working on this project for months. I just had to finish the last bit of material before my presentation on Monday morning. This could mean a really big promotion for me. Personally, I felt like it was long overdue. But for a black woman in the American world of business, the glass ceiling is a lot lower, and it's usually made of cement.

The horn of Jacob's Chevy bellowed outside, and Jackson immediately grabbed his cleats and tried to wiz past me without so much as a quick 'goodbye'. He had almost made it to the door before he decided to turn around and kiss me.

"Bye, Mama," he managed to rattle off as he made a mad dash for the door again.

"Bye, Baby. Have a great game."

I should've left it at that, but something made me walk to the door. I just had to see him off. I saw more than I was prepared for. Jacob was sitting in my driveway with another woman in his truck. All I managed to see was dark skin and long hair.

The angry little black woman raised up and jerked Jackson back into the house before he even made it down the walkway. She began to march toward the Chevy. Jacob quickly jumped out of the truck and stopped her in her tracks.

"Shamonica! Do not make a scene! I told you already how it was going to be."

How dare he attempt to calm me down! And who the hell did he think he was to just tell me how *my* life was gonna be? Finally, I let the angry little black woman speak.

"I know damn well you didn't think I was gonna let my baby go anywhere with you while you're with **her**!"

"First of all, he is not just *your* baby. Jackson is *our* son. Secondly, he should be able to go anywhere with me...and my future wife."

"Well he won't be goin' anywhere with your triflin' ass today! I'll be damned if I let him walk out of my house to ride off with a sorry low life hustler and his damn home wreckin' tramp."

"Was I a low life hustler when you were beggin' me to marry you?"

"How dare you? I have never begged for anything in this life! Everything you are, Jacob, *I* made you! Anything you have that is worth anything, you obtained with **me**.

Just remember that while you're off makin' babies with that bitch!"

"Look, Mo…I didn't come here for this. My son has a game today and I'm going to take him to it. End of discussion."

That was just like Jacob. He was always trying to control the flow of things. I made up my mind he was not getting what he wanted this time. I rushed back into the house and locked the door. I had forgotten Jackson was even in the house let alone standing right at the front door. His sad little eyes looked at me puzzled and confused, waiting for a response of any kind. Those were my eyes he was looking at me through. The same eyes I had just looked at Jacob with just four days earlier.

"Jackson, mommy is gonna take you to your game." I tried to fake a smile. The pain wouldn't let the smile out. All I could manage was tears.

"It's okay, mommy. We don't have to go. I understand."

As he hugged me to comfort me, I knew there was no way he could possibly understand. How could his little 4-year-old mind make sense of what I couldn't even manage to comprehend?

The front door rattled as Jacob tried to fit his key into the lock which I had already had changed. Jackson hurried up the stairs to his bedroom and I heard the door close behind him.

"Shamonica, this is ridiculous! Open the damned door!"

"Jacob, my son is not going anywhere with you! *That's* the way it's going to be!"

"Fine, have it your way! But I will be back on Monday to get my son. I don't intend for him to miss my wedding!"

Did he just say 'wedding'? I know damned well he didn't just say he's getting married on Monday! I felt an entirely different kind of pain at that moment. I tried to move my feet, but they were like lead. I slid down the wall I was standing next to. I ended up on the floor next to Jackson's cleats. I didn't have the strength to move from that spot. So there I laid, thinking to myself that any other day we would have been going to Jackson's game as a family. Jacob cranked up the Chevy, and I heard him back out of the driveway with the radio blaring.

In my miiind...I'll always be his lady...in my miiind...

I was still in the same spot when I heard the front door rattle again. Only this time, the key worked. It was Lena. She had come to check on me because Jackson called her when he ran up to his room.

"Girl, what the hell is wrong with you? Jackson called

and said you and Jacob were over here fightin'!"

"He's gone, Lena." My lips were moving, but barely a whisper was all I could manage.

"What the hell? Did he hit you? I'll kill that bastard! What happened? Where is Jackson?"

It felt like just a few moments since I had heard Jacob drive away, but I knew it had to have been longer. Lena didn't waste any more time on me than she had to. She had one concern in all of this and I knew it. She had come for her nephew.

"Jackson! Jackson! Baby, Tee-tee is here, honey!" She walked up the stairs to his room and found him asleep in his bed with his soccer ball as a pillow.

"Girl, I don't care what you're goin' through with that no good man of yours, but you better get your shit together where my nephews are concerned!" Her words were like sledgehammers hitting me in the head over and over. I didn't know how hard I fell, or how long I had been on the floor, but I knew I had a terrible headache from crying. My eyes were still burning.

"Lena, please," I struggled to lift myself from the spot I was in. "I'm not in the mood for one of your lectures today. Besides, I'm sure you'll be happy to know that he's not my man anymore."

"Mo, what are you talking about? You're not making any sense."

"Jacob. You always said I'd be better off without him. Well, apparently he was listening. He left me. He came over here today trying to pick up Jackson and he had his *fiancée* with him."

"What fiancée? Mo, what the hell is going on? What are you talking about?"

"I wish I knew, Lena. All I know is that he left me on Tuesday, and he says he's getting married this Monday."

"Come on now, Mo. I'm sure you are wrong about at least some of this. I mean I know I give Jacob a hard time, but this sounds crazy even for him."

"I'm just telling you what I know, Lena. I really don't feel like talking about it anymore."

"Well, you may not talk about it to me, but you're gonna talk to somebody. You need to start thinking about your children! If you don't take care of yourself, you can't take care of them. I can call a counselor for you if you would like. We have a really good one at the hospital. She will give you a discount since you're my sister. Of course, everything will be kept totally confidential."

"Do whatever you want, Lena. I just don't see how cryin' on somebody's couch for an hour a week is going to help."

"Well layin' on the floor and cryin' to yourself doesn't seem to be doing anything either. How long have you known about all this? Who have you told?"

"Lena, please! Just let it go. I haven't told anybody because there is nothing anybody can do. I don't feel like hearing all the I-told-you-so's and fake sympathy."

"Well I'll tell you this, little sister. You may not agree with my methods of dealing with Jacob, but I have been here for you every single time he has messed up. I was here when he jacked up your credit. I was here when he wrecked your car. Hell, I was here when you almost lost this house less than a year ago. So don't you try to lecture me on what's real. And don't you dare try to push me away when I can clearly see you need me. There is nothing in the world I wouldn't do for you and those precious little angels of yours. I'm not a mind reader, Mo. If you won't tell me what's going on, how can I possibly help you?"

"Okay, I give. You're right. I'm wrong. So the story goes."

"Mo, this is not about right and wrong. It's about family. Please, just let me help you. Mathieu and Jackson can stay with the girls and me for a few days. At least until you can get your head on straight. They don't need to be around if he comes back anyway. Jackson sounded so scared when he called me he could barely talk. I'll leave it to you to explain to him what happened. I have to draw the line somewhere. You should think about staying at Mama's for a few days to get away, too."

"It's no use, Lena. He'll only come over there looking

for me. You know Mama doesn't need that kind of drama at her house. I'll just have to deal with Jacob my own way."

"Well I'm calling the hospital right now. I think I can get that counselor's cell number. She's seen several of my patients in the past and she'll probably be able to see you today, considering your present circumstances."

"Fine, Lena. I'll go get Jackson and Mathieu's bags. Just don't tell Mama when you go pick up Mathieu. I don't want her worrying about me."

"No offense, Sis, but somebody needs to be worried about you. From what I see you're damn sure not worryin' enough about yourself."

She was right. All that I had done in life was for my kids or my family. I suppose it was time for me to take care of me. The project would just have to wait. I wasn't going to do anything productive that day anyway. I thought going to see a counselor might be good for me. At least she would be someone who didn't know me... or Jacob. I thought maybe she would be able to offer an unbiased view of the situation.

Chapter Three
The Counselor

One thing I can say about Lena is that she is definitely a problem solver. I don't know how she did it, but she convinced this woman to see me on a Saturday with only two hours notice. I didn't even have time to get dressed. I got the boys' bags ready while talking to Jackson about what was going on. I gave him the opportunity to ask a bunch of questions that I had no answers to, and it was time for me to head out to her office. It was a 30 minute drive, but I was hoping it would be worth it. I really didn't know what to expect, though. I had never seen a counselor before. Even after the rape nine years ago I didn't feel like a counselor was really what would help me. I suppose this visit was long overdue. I had been having flashbacks about the assault, and couldn't sleep. Of course, I didn't want to tell Lena or my mother. I felt like none of my friends would be able to understand, either.

I chose to suffer in silence in the hope that the memories would fade with time. What I really wanted to know was what these thoughts had to do with Jacob and why all of this was resurfacing now. I had accepted the fact that the rape was not my fault. I was comfortable with my decision to have Mathieu, and I never looked back. As far as I was concerned, having him was the only thing good that happened during that period in my life. That's why I named him Mathieu. The name means 'a gift from God'. That's just what he was to me. He gave me something else to focus on other than my pain. I guess now it was finally time to pay the piper and deal with all the residue from my past. Could she help me with that?

My thoughts were interrupted by the cartoon-sounding voice of a middle aged white woman. She looked like your typical counselor, dressed in a pair of slacks with a cream-colored shirt and the arms of her sweater tied around her neck. She wore glasses that had the little beaded eyeglass chain, even though I was sure she never took them off.

"She-mi-ca?"

"It's Shamonica."

"Oh, of course! Sorry about that. Well, my name is Rosemary...Rosemary Mitchell." She extended her hand and allowed me to shake her fingers. Now maybe it's the businesswoman in me, but I hate a weak handshake. This was just as much a business deal as anything else as far as I was concerned. I was paying her a fee for a service. Didn't she know the proper etiquette for the exchange?

I spent the next 30 minutes filling out paperwork and insurance forms. She even had the nerve to ask for the co-payment upfront. I was expecting us to just get right down to the counseling. I was even more upset by the time all the preliminary stuff was over with. The only reason I didn't walk right out of there was because I knew she was doing this as a favor to Lena. I was trying to focus on the fact that I needed help. Actually, I was focusing on the fact that I was *told* I needed help. As far as I was concerned, there was nothing a fifth of Hennessy and a can of coke wouldn't solve. Finally, she invited me into her office which was filled with colorful lamps and pictures of flowers and butterflies. She even had colorful couch covers and stuffed animals all over the place. I felt like I had walked into a twisted excerpt from a bad children's movie. Nonetheless, I managed to find a seat in the corner of the room. I sat down next to a stuffed raccoon who seemed to want to be rescued from this bad dream as much as I did.

"So, She-manda..."

"It's Sha-MON-I-CA," I tried to keep the angry little black woman polite, but I could tell she was just waiting for the opportunity to show out.

"Yes, well...tell me a little about what's going on with

you today. Your sister said you were pretty upset when
she called."

"Well, basically, I'm going through a break-up and I
suppose it's more difficult than I thought it would be. My
common law husband of almost five years has informed
me that not only is he leaving me, but he's also having a
baby with another woman and they're getting married on
Monday. I haven't been able to focus very well on work
or any other daily activities. Also, I'm having trouble
sleeping. Just two days ago I started having flashbacks
about an assault that occurred nine years ago." I was
surprised at how the words flowed so freely. I figured
maybe this was not such a bad thing. Maybe I needed
talk about all of this in a calm, rational manner. I hadn't
actually spoken the words until today. Maybe this was
what I needed. Just to talk it all out.

"I see...assault...boyfriend left you..." She was jotting
down notes as she rattled off each item like a shopping
list. "So, Shemangum, tell me more about the assault.
Was it someone you knew? Did you seek counseling after
the event?"

"I was raped when I was 23. I was out with some
girlfriends. They decided to stay at the club we had gone
to, and I wanted to go home. I was abducted from a bus
stop, and that's when the assault occurred. A few months
later I found out I was pregnant with my first son." I didn't

know what had happened, but as I was stating the story in a matter-of-fact type manner, my face got hot. I felt my eyes burn with tears that I'm sure had been in hiding for years. I felt dizzy, and my hands and feet began to tingle and they felt numb. I would learn later that I had experienced an anxiety attack.

"Okay, Shemika, now listen to me. I need you to take slo-o-ow, de-e-ep breaths. Picture all the bad energy flowing out of your fingertips and out through your toes. Just bre-e-athe in deep and let the positive energy flo-o-w from your belly out to the rest of your body." What the hell was she talking about! It was all I could do to keep myself breathing at all. And why was it so hard for her to get my damn name right! I had no time to think about that. I buried my head in my hands and began to plot how I was going to kill Lena for making me come here…just as soon as I could catch my breath. I would deal with Rosemary Poppins later.

"I'm okay. I just need a moment." I tried to maintain as much of my composure as I could. I know how bad I must have looked. There I sat in my sweats and an old tee shirt that read 'Mean People Suck'. I was crying my eyes out and sniffling like a little child with no one to comfort me but a stuffed raccoon and a woman who, I swear, looked like the grandmother from the Tweety bird cartoon. It was time for me to go.

"Shemika? Shemika!" She was really pushing it with the name thing.

"I *said* I'm okay." I used the firmest tone I could find without cursing.

"Well, that's pretty much all the time we have today, but I would definitely like to see you on Tuesday." *I'll bet you would.* That $100 an hour was an ample incentive for her to see me every Tuesday.

I quickly grabbed my bag and left the building without even so much as another weak handshake from the woman. She scheduled our next appointment for Tuesday afternoon. I figured I had enough time to call and cancel before then without her charging me for the visit anyway. As I left her office, all I could think about was Jacob. How could he have done this to me? Why now? He knew how hard I had worked on this presentation. He was the one who encouraged me to ask for the promotion in the first place. He had put just as much time into this project as I had. All the nights I had to work late, he kept the boys. He had been my support. Whenever I had to go to a meeting early, he always made sure the boys were out to daycare and school on time. Whenever I didn't have the energy to cook when I got home, he assured me everything was under control. He had even cooked a couple of times. I'll never forget the night I came home and Mathieu had diarrhea from one of those authentic African dishes

Jacob had made for him. I guess Jacob's system had also adjusted to American food. Jacob and Mathieu were in the bathroom all night. I was on night watch with Jackson because he hadn't quite figured out how to make it to the bathroom that quickly yet. We decided it was best for Jacob to order out from then on.

We were a family then. I was trying to wrap my mind around how he could just rip all that away in a few days. I mean I'm not totally clueless. I know there had to be signs that I overlooked all this time, but where were they? Jacob had just told me that he was more in love with me now than he had ever been. We were even planning to take a family cruise this summer right after Mathieu finished out the school year.

I began to go over all the mistakes that were made in the relationship. I knew we had moved way too quickly in the beginning. I was just working my way through all the hang-ups I had about dating and men in general. Jacob seemed to be just what I needed, though. I didn't try to trap him by having Jackson, either. I told him that if he wanted to separate and just be parents I was okay with that. He insisted that I was the woman for him and that we were his family. He even accepted Mathieu without question. What did I overlook? How did I allow this woman to steal everything that I had worked so hard to build? What was it she had that I didn't? Why was Jacob so sure about marrying her when he had been with me for five years and most nights he couldn't even make up his mind what he wanted for dinner? I needed answers. I wasn't going to get them talking to Mother Goose, either. I knew what I had to do.

Chapter Four
Naji

Naji was actually more Lena's friend than she was mine. We mostly just saw each other at family events and parties that Jacob and I threw at our place. We liked each other, but we never really hung out the way she and Lena did. I knew that if anyone knew what was going on, it would be Naji. Even though she hadn't talked that much about Jacob in those early days, she was very close to her brother. I could never prove it, but I really think Lena was the reason I didn't meet Jacob sooner back then. She and Naji were close. Naji must've mentioned something to her about him. Maybe Lena even met him or something. Whatever the case was, this was five years later and it was time for me to get the truth…from somebody.

I was a bit nervous as I approached the walkway to Naji's home. I was sure she knew about everything that had been going on. How could she not know that her brother was getting married in a few days? What I wasn't sure about was how open she would be with me about the subject. I didn't know if she would want to talk to me at all. She opened the door before I even rang the doorbell.

"Sha-mon-i-ca, sis-stah! I have been awaiting your arrival!" Her accent was much thicker than that of her brother. I found out shortly after knowing Jacob that he could pretty much turn it off and on at his own discretion. He had been in the states for years before Naji arrived. He associated with a lot of black American men. I guess he just adapted to his surroundings.

She greeted me with a kiss, but requested that I move my car from the front of the house to the back driveway. I knew she must have something to tell me. I felt both relieved and afraid. Was I even ready to hear what she had to say?

"Come in! You look exhausted. I have heard what happened between you and my brotha. Let me tell you right now that I do not approve!" Her long braids were waving as she spoke and shook her head. She waved her thin finger in the air to make her point. As I looked around her home, I began to notice differences between her place and mine. I had expected to see all the African art and sculptures, but what gripped my attention were the pictures. Jacob had never brought pictures of his family to our home. Naji had photos of aunts and uncles, even cousins back home from every visit she had made to Africa. Jacob had never even put up so much as a photo of his mother. Not that I would have approved of her picture in my home anyway, but I just never thought about it. I had pictures of Lena and my mom and dad. Of course we had family photos with Jacob and me with the boys. Never once, though, had we hung photos of any of his family members in Africa.

"Hi, Naji. How've you been?" *Do I just come right out and ask her what I want to know? What is it that I want to know anyway?* She sensed my hesitation and my confusion. I suppose she decided to put me out of my misery.

"I know why you are here. You want to know if I know about the woman my brother has been dating. All I can tell you is that she came here from Nigeria four months ago. To my knowledge, they have been seeing one another ever since." Four months? That's even longer than I've been working on this project for my job. I've been really busy with work lately. Jacob has been doing double duty with the boys. How had he had time to date anyone? Once again my face must've looked perplexed.

"Shemonica, Jacob has been dropping the boys off with me at least once or twice a week for the last month. I assumed you knew since you had been working so late. I never knew when he was going to see her or when he just needed a break. I told him that I did not approve of what he was doing. When I threatened to tell you the truth, he accused me of betraying my family for an outsider. I told him you were just as much family to me as my nephew. I felt that if he wanted to be rid of you, he should tell you so. He told me to mind my own business. You must believe me. I never thought he would do something like this. My brother loves you. I saw the way he looked at you when you two met. I have never seen him look at a woman that way. His eyes do not light up like that when he is with her. I think he has only chosen her because it is more acceptable."

I felt sick to my stomach. My head was spinning with all the new thoughts and questions now. What did she mean by more acceptable? How did she know how he looked at this other woman? Had he brought her around his family? If so, when? Had Jacob brought her around my children? Why didn't Mathieu say something to me? How could I be so blind and foolish?

"Naji, I'm not understanding something. You say that she has been here for four months. Did she come here just for him? Jacob has only been dropping the boys off over here for a few weeks. How did they manage to see each other before then? And why would Jacob have to worry about what's acceptable? Acceptable to whom?" Then it hit me. "Naji, does your mother know about all this?"

Now Naji telling me things about her brother was

one thing, but I knew she would definitely not cross her mother. Jacob's mother was a strong woman who ruled her household with a matriarchal type strength that made a lioness look like an ordinary house cat. If she wanted something for her family, she would do anything to get it. Even if it meant a couple of people had to be rolled over in the process.

Naji didn't have to say a word to me. Her downcast eyes and sad expression told it all. I knew that Jacob's mother had never approved of our relationship. She said it was shameful that I had a child out of wedlock before I met her son. I didn't bother telling her the circumstances under which Mathieu was conceived. It was none of her business. If I knew her like I think I did, it wouldn't have made a difference anyway. She always said she wanted her son to marry a nice Nigerian girl. Even when I bore Jacob's first son, her grandchild, she still never accepted me. Jackson could come by whenever he wanted, but she always looked at me with hatred and contempt in her eyes. She didn't even try to be civil when I allowed her to live in my home. Jacob and Naji were having a house built for her. Jacob and I had just moved into our house, and Naji had not yet purchased one for herself. Naji's studio apartment was much too small for both she and her mother to live in comfortably. I figured the time Jacob's mother would stay with us would give her time to get to know me better. Maybe she'd even like me. I was so wrong.

It took four months and ten days for them to finish the house. I know down to the day because I was ready to move out myself had it been just one more hour. She made my life a living hell the entire time she was there. I drew the line one night when I caught her showing favoritism toward Jackson. He and Mathieu were playing with some toys that Jacob had brought back from his last visit to Africa. She told Mathieu that he would have to wait for Jackson to pick the toy he wanted to play with first and then take what was left over. She told him that his brother was a prince, but that he could not be one because he didn't come from the proper bloodline. The angry little black woman went off on that rusty old battle-ax that night. Had it not been for Jacob coming in when he did, things would have certainly gotten physical. It was then that I informed him that as soon as her house was finished, she was no longer welcome in mine. I assumed she shared the same sentiment. I did her the honor of never darkening her doorstep. If I even saw her number on the caller ID I would let Jacob answer. If he wasn't home, I would let the call go to voice mail. All in all, I thought we had a mutual respect for one another. I expected her to mind her own damn business, and she felt the same toward me. Apparently I underestimated her hatred for me somehow. I still knew there was no way she could've done this on her own. She didn't have the money that it would've taken to fly this woman here. Somebody had to be helping her. Naji was fearful enough to do it, but she didn't have that kind of money to just throw around, either. There were at least ten other possible ways this could've happened.

Jacob came from a large family. There were twelve children in all. Some were still in Nigeria, but there were eight of them living either in the U.S. or in Europe. His mother kept a tight rein on them all. She was especially particular about her sons. There were nine girls and three boys. Jacob was the youngest male. He was also the only brother who was not married. He and his brothers had helped to put Naji through school. Now she could support herself and help her mother out here and there. She was able to help Jacob with the down payment on her mother's house with the sign on bonus from her first job as a registered nurse. Later, she built her own house with money she had been saving by living in a small studio apartment where the rent was probably less than the light bill every month. If there were ever anything good I could say about Jacob's mother, it would be that she raised a group of strong men and women. All of Jacob's siblings now had the ability to support themselves. Naji was the baby girl. Now that she was on her own, I figured Jacob's mother would have been done raising her children. Once again I was wrong.

I would sit in Naji's living room for another six hours before she finished telling me what had been going on. The other woman's name was Salihah. She had been living with Jacob's mother since just before Christmas. It made perfect sense to me, because that was around that time that Jacob and I began having problems. He began to spend more and more time at his mother's and less at home. He told me that she was ill and wanted him to be around to help out more. I had noticed that she was calling a lot more and the one time I did choose to answer the phone, her voice sounded weak. I had intended to confront her about all the extra time she had been requiring of Jacob. I wanted to tell her that our bond was strong and that I refused to allow her to break us apart. I heard the weakness in her voice as she asked for the only son she had near her, and I couldn't bring myself to pick a fight with her in that state. I remember thinking that even she must have *some* limits. I laugh at myself now. She had no respect for me or the family that I had built. She only cared about keeping her family the way she wanted it. In the end, I guess it wasn't up to me to stay with Jacob. It was his choice to abandon me. There was nothing I could do about that.

I spent the Christmas holidays with my family. The

boys went with me, and Jacob went to his mother's. What I didn't know was that, while Jacob was at his mother's, Salihah was already assuming the role of daughter-in-law. This was not their first time meeting. Kumani, Jacob's mother, had arranged for them to meet during one of his visits to Africa. I didn't go with him because I was still pregnant with Jackson. He planned to be gone for four weeks. This meant he would be back about two weeks before my due date. He planned to tell his mother about the pregnancy during that visit. Kumani knew he had been dating someone, but she had no idea we were so serious about one another. Salihah was apparently the daughter of a wealthy family in Nigeria. Kumani had used her influence to convince the girl's father that she would be perfect for Jacob. Apparently, Jacob tried to resist the meeting at first. Naji said that Jacob had told her of the meeting at the time and that he was insulted that his mother would be so disrespectful of his relationship with me. He tried to convince his mother that he was in love with a wonderful woman here in the states. Once he told her I was pregnant she told him to keep quiet. She said that he must never mention me or my baby in her home again. Jacob never told me any of this when he returned. I don't know if he was ashamed of his mother, or ashamed of me.

In any event, his mother moved to the U.S. a few years later. She was staying in a small apartment that was paid for by her children. Her son in Europe sent money every week, and Jacob helped out with anything extra she might need. Their other brother was much older and lived in the U.S. as well. He sent money when he could, but he had a daughter who was about to enter college. Plus, he was still helping Naji to get the things she needed.

Naji told me that she didn't hear anymore about Salihah until she and Jacob were having the house built. It was then that her mother began plotting to have Jacob marry Salihah. She had promised that she would move Salihah to the U.S. as soon as her son had finished building *his* house. That old bat had everything planned to a tee. That was why she was so evil toward me in my own home. She figured I was on borrowed time. I guess she was right.

Naji also told me Salihah's father had been sending money to help with Jacob's new shop. I guess it was some kind of dowry. Jacob had been telling me that business was good and that he was making more money at the shop. Apparently, his newfound father-in-law was the reason why he could afford all the new equipment and things. We even had new stuff around the house. He bought the new high-tech washer and dryer I had been lusting after. I had hinted around for weeks that I wanted them. I was just happy to see him making more of a contribution.

I had carried us when we first moved into our home. He had just opened the shop, and I didn't expect it to be an overnight success. I expected to have to take care of much of the household expenses. Lena helped me out last year when things really got rough and I thought we were going to lose the house. After putting all I had into helping Jacob with the shop, I figured the return should be more than enough to keep us afloat. The problem with those kinds of investments is that you never know how fast or how slow the return will be. Ever since Christmas, though, Jacob said business was picking up. I thought it was a bit odd, but who questions money? Now I know the questions I should have been asking.

Naji talked to me until I felt my head about to burst open. She said that Jacob had to marry Salihah now whether he wanted to or not. Her father had no idea about the pregnancy. I asked how she knew that. She said it was because Jacob was still alive. Her mother would not have him disgrace her by not marrying this girl after her father had entrusted her to them. She said he had been playing with fire for a long time. The wedding should have been months ago, but Jacob kept giving excuses for why he couldn't go through with it. Salihah's father demanded that his daughter be sent home, and Jacob finally gave in. Naji said that Jacob didn't even tell her about the pregnancy until this week.

"Shamonica, I told him he had to tell you immediately to spare you any more heartache. I know it was only a small gesture, but I can not control my brother's choices in life. I only attempt to guide him in the right direction." Her eyes began to fill with tears. For the first time in four days I felt like somebody finally understood some of my pain.

"None of this is your fault, Naji. Jacob is an adult. He has made choices that will affect all of us for the rest of our lives. I just hope that he can deal with the bed he's made for himself."

"He does not love her, Shamonica. He cannot. He gave you his heart a long time ago. It is impossible for him to take that back."

"Naji, I don't think Jacob loves anyone but himself. But thank you for your kind words. Don't worry about me telling your mother or Jacob about this conversation. As far as I'm concerned it never happened. You take care of yourself. I wish you and your family the best...all of you."

I left her house that evening not even knowing how I felt. Physically, I was a wreck. My head hurt, I was nauseated, and I kept having that tingling feeling in my hands and feet. However, hearing all that stuff was a mental relief in a strange kind of way. It was like I had been given the key to a new door that I didn't even know existed. I didn't know what to do with it, but I just felt somehow empowered. She had given me the answers that I knew I would never have gotten from Jacob. Now it was up to me to figure out what my next move would be.

Chapter Five
Jada

I could only do one thing after my visit with Naji. Sleep. I managed to hop in and out of the shower before I fell onto my king sized bed in a heap of miserable exhaustion. I dozed off while still on top of the covers. I didn't really dream much while lying there, but I did think. For some reason, the situation became almost bearable while I was sleeping. I could actually think about it as if I wasn't involved. It felt more like being on the outside looking in. I didn't even care that the love of my life was getting married to another woman and they were going to have a –

Ring......ring.......ring!

I answered the phone without even opening my eyes. The voice on the other end was even more startling than the ring itself.

"Girl, get yo' ass up! I know you are not layin' in

that bed tryin' to feel sorry for yourself! I'm on my way over there, so you better pick out an outfit and some CFM's. I'm not lettin' you make me late, and I'm not going without you. Bye!"

That was Jada. She needed no introduction and no invitation. It was a good thing, too, 'cause she very rarely waited for either one. Jada had been with me basically my whole life. We graduated from pre-school together and have shared every other graduation since. We purposely attended separate colleges and tried to race each other to the finish line. We still ended up graduating at the same time. Friends like that are hard to come by. I knew without asking that Lena have given her the dish on what was happening with Jacob and me. I would have to fill in the blanks for her later. Tonight she was on a mission. CFM was Jada's term for a sexy pair of shoes: basically, a pair of shoes that just screamed, "Come fuck me!" Anytime she said to break out the CFM's, it could only mean one thing. Jada was on a manhunt.

I was just starting to get dressed when I heard her banging on the front door. She would have normally just walked right in, but she didn't have a key yet. Lena was the only one I had given a key to when I changed the locks. It was only because I saw her at my mother's house that same day. I grabbed my robe and ran down the front stairs. The house phone was ringing and Jada was leaving me a message cursing me out for still being asleep just as I opened the front door.

"You woman enough to say that to my face?" I gave a smug grin as I opened the door and stepped aside.

"Girl, please! You couldn't even whip me when we were kids. I'm a grown ass woman! What you gon' do with all this?"

Jada spun around with her arms in the air. Partly to boast of her fabulous figure, and partly to show me her outfit which I knew without asking that she had just bought. She had been working out vigorously for the last 6 months and it showed.

"All that time you've been spendin' in the gym has strained your memory muscle. I used to kick your butt when we were kids."

"That was just because I didn't want to break my nails. You know I always was the cute one."

Jada was right. She had always been one of the prettiest black women I knew. She was a chocolate sister with almond shaped eyes. We used to tease her and say that she was blackanese when we were in school. She had full lips that didn't overtake her face. As a matter of fact, her smile was one of her best features. Her long hair would change in color according to what season it was. She dyed it, permed it, twisted it, braided it, but she refused to ever cut it. She would always say that her hair was the best accessory God could've given her. She had always been a bit on the heavy side, but all that changed when we went to college. She had never been fat as far as I was concerned. Brothers used to always say she was thick. Plus, she had really large breasts. It just fit that she should have hips and thighs to match. The freshman fifteen hit her hard, though. She vowed never to be that heavy again. She wasn't necessarily a fitness buff, but she tried to stay healthy. The last six months had been a bit different, though. Jada had a pretty close scare with an episode of chest pain about eight months ago. Even though everything turned out to be okay, it was enough to scare her into a fitness frenzy. She stopped working as much overtime and started spending more time in the gym. I must admit that I was a bit jealous. She was standing in front of me with toned arms, a tight tummy, and legs that only Tina Turner would be able to compete with. The girl was bad. I had to give her props.

"Girl, get yo' ass in this house before you have every man on my block beatin' my door down. You've probably already been stoppin' traffic the whole way here!"

"Hey, at least I've got on clothes. You're the one standin' here givin' the strip tease."

"Careful there, sista. You *barely* have clothes on."

The atmosphere was light as we made our way up to my bedroom. We both knew eventually we would have to talk about Jacob. If I knew Jada, it would be after we both had a few drinks in us. This was our time to just be us. Two single young women getting ready for a night out. No responsibilities and no worries. I liked that. For one moment, I was able to relax. I felt like a child who was getting ready to go on a field trip. I already had my outfit on the bed. I had made it a habit to never get dressed before going out with Jada because she normally picked out something else for me anyway. Once again, she did not disappoint me.

"Girl, I said we were goin' *clubin'*, not *churchin'*! What is this?"

She made a face as she picked up the little black dress on my bed. We both knew full well that this dress was more than appropriate for where we were going. Jada just liked to think that less was more where clothes were concerned. I didn't mind most of the time, but tonight I was not in a mood to be hit on. I just wanted to go out and relax with my girl.

"Look, Mama, I've been dressing myself for a few years now —"

"Yes I know," She interrupted, "and I'm here to rescue you from this mangled fashion accident you call a closet."

"Oh, no you didn't!" I protested.

Jada darted back down the stairs and came back up

with two boxes. One was a shoe box and the other was a big box with a bow.

"Girl, I knew you weren't gonna rise to the occasion. No offense, Mo, but I can't be seen with you lookin' anything less than fabulous!"

I rolled my eyes as I opened the first box. It was a short black dress with the back out. The neck had sequins around it and hooked in the back. It looked like it was the only piece of fabric to hold the thing up. In the second box was a silver pair of shoes that were definitely worth of the CFM stamp of approval. Jada was trying to make me feel better. She knew I loved new stuff.

I picked out my make-up quickly and applied it even quicker. I sat at my vanity and Jada just watched as I transformed myself into a new creature. One who looked less tired and worn. We didn't talk. There would be time for that later. As I headed for my walk-in closet to put the dress on, I couldn't help feeling like a little girl who had just gotten a new Easter dress. An Easter dress this was not. I could hardly believe how good the thing looked on me. *Hell, I would want to hit on me if I saw me in this!* I emerged from the closet slowly, but with confidence. I knew how good I looked. I just couldn't believe it.

"Ooh, girl!" Jada couldn't hide her own amazement at how well my body took to this fabric. "Now that's what I'm talkin' about! Hell, where you been hidin' all that at anyway?"

"I wish I knew."

I looked in the mirror and saw a beautiful woman in a beautiful dress, but I couldn't help feeling that outside-looking-in feeling again. How could I be so wonderfully beautiful on the outside when inside all I felt was hurt? I looked into the eyes of the woman in the mirror and tried to see if she could feel what I felt. There it was. Hidden deep behind the beautiful round eyes of hers was the pain of a woman who had given nothing but devotion and admiration to a man who didn't appreciate any of it. I gave her one last look and quickly proclaimed.

"Fuck him! I am too cute and too damn fine to be puttin' up with his bullshit anyway."

"You say somethin' Mo'?"

Jada was in my bathroom raiding my perfume counter as was her normal routine. I quickly slipped my perfectly pedicured toes into the shoes Jada had lain at the foot of the bed.

"Nah, girl, let's go."

I took one last look at myself before I walked out. I just wanted to be sure the lady in the mirror knew I meant what I had said. She nodded back, but her eyes were still sad behind the silver glow of the eye shadow I had chosen. I decided she and I would come to agreement later. Right now it was time to have fun.

Chapter Six
G.Q.

Jada always did know how to party. Even when we were teenagers, she was the friend who always knew where to go. I was always the one who was brave enough and smart enough to sneak us out of the house to get there. We were a perfect team. Tonight was no different. Jada had a spot in mind that was usually for a younger crowd. This night, however, they were throwing a birthday party. Apparently some friends that she worked with knew the guest of honor.

"Your friend must be pretty rich, girl. They shut down an entire club just for his birthday?"

I was really just trying to make conversation. Usually, the silence between us was okay, but the closer we got to the club, I could almost hear the clock ticking down to the time I would have to say something about my situation.

"Girl, please, I told you I don't know him. This was just the place to be tonight. You know me. I never miss a party."

"Well just the same, thanks for coming to get me. I appreciate the chance to get out of the house. Work has just taken up so much of my time lately. Between this new project, the boys, and Jacob…" *Damn it! Why did I say his name?*

Jada immediately sensed my displeasure at the taste of his name in my mouth.

"Girl, how are the boys doing anyway? Didn't Jackson have a soccer game this weekend?"

"Yeah, he did. You know he's one of the best kids on the team, not that I'm biased or anything." We shared a nervous laugh before Jada proceeded.

"Mo', you know you can always talk to me. I don't want to pry, though, so I won't. When you're ready to let it all out, I know you will. You always have been the strong one. I'm always blubberin' and whining to you about something. Well now I'm asking you to take advantage of your turn. You don't have to be strong for everybody. Not for me anyway. It's okay to just be Mo'. I can't even imagine how you must feel. I'm still in shock from just hearing about part of it, and it's not even happening to me. I can't force you to talk. I can't even say I'll know exactly what to say when you do. What I can do is be here. That's just what I intend to do. Know that whenever you need me I'm here. Day or night you just say the word. Now if you're not feelin' this party tonight —"

"Girl, please!" I interrupted. "Do you know how long it's been since I've been out? Hell, I *need* this! What I don't need is to keep feeling like I'm less of a woman just because Jacob was too blind or too heartless to recognize who I really am. You know, in the end that's all this is about. If he had left me for a reason, I would be able to deal with it. But he didn't. Truth be told, he didn't even leave me for another woman. He left me for a fantasy. Matter of fact, it's not even his. This is about some damn idea his mother has of the way he is *supposed* to live his life. Well damn her! Damn her and damn him for listening to her, Jada! I am too good for this shit! I don't deserve to be treated this way, and if he thinks for one minute that I'm just going to sit quietly and let this go off without a hitch, he's got another thing coming!"

The silence in the car after my outburst was deafening. My ears rang with the echoes of my unspoken questions. My heart silently pleaded. Why wouldn't he just love me? What would be so hard about that? The pounding had started again in my chest. I could feel my eyes burning behind the silver clouds I had painted over the window shades of my soul. I closed my eyes and refused to allow the tears to escape. I took a deep breath as I prepared to break the heaviness I had brought upon us.

"Girl, park this damn car so I can get a drink. You see I'm losin' it over here! Tell the bartender to get me an apple martini with a double shot of Valium."

We both roared with laughter. The joke had not been that funny, but we were both just relieved to be able to laugh at a time like this. Sometimes laughter is the cure for what ails you. Although this was not one of those times, we both intended to take all the healing we could from this moment. We pulled up in front of the club and Jada handed the keys to the valet none too soon for me. The line wasn't as long as I expected. It seemed like we were at the door in a matter of seconds.

Once we got inside, I was half relieved to be out of the house, but half feeling like maybe I shouldn't have come. There were people there who looked like they should be in somebody's classroom instead of a club. Girls were prancing around in dresses that looked like underwear. Guys were dressed in anything from linen suits to dress shirts and slacks. One guy even had on a tailored suit. The acne on his face made me think he had probably borrowed it from his dad. I was just glad there wasn't any denim allowed. I swear if I had seen just one person in those sagging blue jeans I would have run out of there screaming. I don't mind the changes fashion makes over time. As a matter of fact, I normally consider myself to be quite a trendy person. That was just one fashion I couldn't adjust to. I mean why would a grown ass man want to run around showin' his butt all the time? It annoys me to even see them at the supermarket pulling their jeans up over and over. Once I shouted at one guy, "Hey! It's called a belt! Make an investment, smarty pants!" I guess I'm lucky he didn't curse me out, but I just couldn't help it. That bugs the hell out of me.

It's a good thing there was more than one level inside. Jada and I pushed passed the pediatric floor and went upstairs in search of some grown folk. There were four floors in all, but she and I decided to stop on the second one. There was music that we were comfortable with, and even men who looked like they wouldn't get Jada arrested for taking them home. I knew she would go sightseeing upstairs later. Jada just has an adventurous nature. All I needed to do was find a good seat and a good bartender. I hurried to the bar for my apple martini. Jada and I quickly found a seat in a corner where I figured I wouldn't be bothered. She just wanted to get a better look at the entire room before making out her dance card. Neither plan worked. No sooner than our butts hit the seats, a guy who looked way too young for her had already grabbed Jada's hand and whisked her onto the dance floor. I politely declined an invite from his friend just to be approached by two other brothers during the same song. I lied the same lie all three times.

"This just isn't my type of music. Maybe you can catch me later."

Each brother seemed to sense the insincerity in my tone and quietly walked away. None seemed fazed by the rejection at all. I guess people have become so used to fakeness and insincerity that it wouldn't have mattered what I said. That's when it hit me. I was really single. I was back out on the dating scene and going to be subject to all the madness that went with it. My thoughts were interrupted before I could plummet into the true depression that I was on my way to.

"Is this seat taken?" The first things I saw were his shoes. They were just like a pair I had recently bought for Jacob. I had splurged on them, so I knew how expensive they were. I was breathless for a moment. I knew the man filling these shoes couldn't be him, but I was just taken aback momentarily. My eyes made their way up to a cream colored suit. Underneath was a light blue shirt with the top two buttons undone. I recognized the suit from the new Todd Smith line that was to be released in a couple of months. My company had a contract with one of the distributors.

I must've looked startled. He attempted to start over and began to introduce himself.

"Hello. My name is Gerald. Gerald Quinton Adams.

My friends call me G.Q."

"Hello, Gerald," I grunted ignoring his extended hand.

"I've been watching you turn down every guy who asked you to dance, so I figured I'd try to talk to you first. You look like you could use a friend."

"Well the last friend I had fucked somebody, got her pregnant, and they're getting married the day after tomorrow. Excuse me if I don't seem to have much faith in the institution of *friendship* at the moment!"

I shocked myself with the psycho-bitch response. I had meant to sound harsh, but dang! That was a lot. I sipped my drink to hide my own disbelief at what had just spewed out of my mouth.

"Well, sounds to me like you had a little boy when what you were really looking for was a man." He sat down. "Can I freshen your drink?"

I almost choked on my martini. What the hell was he doing? Didn't he just hear me? And who told him he could sit down anyway?

"No. I'm fine."

I looked at him for the first time and felt a chill go through me. He had eyes like my dad. They were hazel and almost looked fake in the flashing lights of the club. There was something warm about them, though. I couldn't release myself from his stare. His face was absolutely perfect. He looked like an artist had chiseled every detail into place. His broad shoulders were sitting atop a chest that looked like a cross between L.L. Cool J and the Rock. I felt like Superman must feel every time he is near kryptonite. I knew this was just what I didn't need. Any other time, I might have been flattered by attention from a man that fine. Tonight, however, was not the night.

"Well, Ms. Lady, since you're fine, maybe you can walk with me while I get my drink."

"Excuse me?"

"I just figured that as good as you look in that dress, you should give the room a better view. I mean, nobody else in here is that fine. Give the brothers a break. If you're not gonna strut it on the dance floor, at least take a spin around the room."

"Look, Mr. Adams. I don't know what you're used to, but whatever it is, that's what this is *not*. I'm flattered by the attention. You have made a gallant effort to woo me. It's not working. Good-bye. Have a nice night."

"Wow!" His eyes widened in a fake surprised gesture. "You're tough. You almost had me convinced to walk away from this table. I don't know where you got your acting skills from, but they are good." His chuckle was almost insulting.

"Acting?" I frowned with displeasure at his obviously

correct assessment of the situation.

"Yes! I said acting. I mean come on, you come in here looking like a diva in a haystack of hood rats and then act like you expected to sit here alone in a corner and not be bothered. You had to know somebody was gonna approach you. As a matter of fact, I think you came here just for me tonight."

"What the —" My sentence was interrupted as he continued as if what I had to say couldn't possibly matter.

"What I mean is that I believe it fate. I know I was supposed to meet you here tonight. I have had a feeling all day that something special was going to happen to me."

I gave him a fake applause.

"That's it. I give up. You have figured me out Mr. Adams. I suppose now we can do the wedding thing and have those 2.2 kids everybody's always talkin' about. By the way, we're only 0.2 short. Oh, and I already have a house. I don't care much for picket fences. I suppose my privacy fence will suffice. Oh, and silly me, would you like to know my name before we go any further?"

I was really impressed with how well I had this psycho-bitch thing down. He was right. My acting skills were excellent. He, however, was still not buying it.

"I already know your name, Shamonica." My eyes must've widened with more shock than I thought. "Oh, you're surprised? Or did they teach you that expression in acting class, as well?"

"How did you—"

"I saw you outside in line and asked the bouncer to get me your name when you came in."

"Well it's a good thing you got my name tonight. I'm going back home tomorrow. Maybe you can stalk me some other time if I return to town."

"Well, I shouldn't have any problems with that. Aaron says you live on the north side."

My jaw dropped in amazement.

"I didn't ask him that part, I think he was just lookin' for a bigger tip." He gave me another chuckle that made me wonder what else he was going to drop on me later.

"Did he also give you my driver's license number and make and model of my car? Perhaps a criminal background check?"

"Well, it actually takes 48 hours for those things to come back. I was hoping you would be willing to tell me anything else I needed to know." His smile was beautiful. Nice full, soft lips encircled his straight white teeth. He even had a dimple on one side of his face. It was odd. I liked that.

"And what exactly would you like to know, Mr. Adams?" I sat back and allowed my expression to soften. It was obvious that he had no plans of walking away without getting what he had come here for...whatever that was.

"I want to know everything. For instance, why is someone as beautiful as you single? I want to know how to contact you after tonight. I also want you to have full access to me whenever you want."

"Full access, huh?" The only thing I heard in my mind was the word 'kryptonite'. It was like my whole body went limp. I was intoxicated by the smell of the man's cologne, but all I wanted to do was loose myself from his stare. I didn't know what kind of voodoo he was working, but I was not doing a good job of resisting it.

He grabbed my hand and kissed it. He didn't let it go. Instead, he got up and led me away from the table. We walked all the way up to the fourth level of the club where there was a large booth in the corner. There was already a bottle of champagne on the table chilling. He led me to the inside of the circular booth where there was an apple martini already in place. It was like he had been waiting for me.

"You don't really think I'm going to drink that do you?" I tried to keep my edge, but I must admit I was very impressed with his method.

"Of course, not, that's my drink." He lied. "I was going to let you order what you wanted when you got here."

"So you knew I would be here, then."

"Well, Shamonica, I have a bit of a confession. See, I tend to be very spoiled. I'm used to always getting what I want."

"And what is it that you want from me Mr. Adams?"

"I just want a little time to get to know you. After that, you are free to continue whatever plans you had this evening. Although, it looks like it will be a while before your girlfriend joins you again."

I looked over the edge of the balcony and could see the entire third level from up there. I saw Jada on the dance floor just below us. She was having the time of her life dancing with man after man. She probably hadn't even had time to get a drink. I was always the drinker. She just got a natural buzz from collecting phone numbers and attention from unsuspecting male patrons. I was content to leave her alone for now. Though I could never admit it to Gerald, I was actually enjoying talking to him. I let him go on the entire evening asking me question after question. It was nice to have someone take an interest in me...my work...my life. He offered very little information other than to say that he was a bit of an entrepreneur and that he owned several small businesses. He didn't get around to telling me what kind of businesses. We talked more about his personal life than anything. He said he had broken up with his fiancée a year ago. He caught her cheating and that was that. He hadn't had a serious relationship since. I didn't offer any more specifics about my situation with Jacob. Partly because I didn't feel like talking about it, and partly because I was still a bit embarrassed about my earlier outburst. We talked for a couple of hours before I became aware of the time.

"Well, Gerald, it's been really nice talking to you, but it's really late. I think I should probably be going now."

"I can respect that. I just want to ask one favor before you go."

"What's that?"

"I want to know I'll be able to talk to you later. Maybe somewhere a little more private and a lot more quiet." I gave him my best I'm-not-that-kind-of-girl look. "Not like that, Shamonica. I'm serious. You intrigue me. There really is something about you that has me drawn to you. Why do you think I went to all this trouble just to be alone with you this evening?"

"I thought you say it was fate that did all this. That means it shouldn't have been any trouble at all for you."

"Okay, okay. Maybe you have a point there. In any event, I still want to speak to you again." He handed me his card. I never even looked at it. I just shoved it into my purse. Some guy had escorted Jada to our table as if he had been cued to do so.

"I'll try to give you a call later in the week, Mr. Adams."

I was trying to regain the same icy edge I had a few hours earlier. I was failing miserably.

"Aaron here will escort you ladies to your car." Gerald was motioning toward the guy with Jada. I recognized him as the bouncer from the door.

"That's okay," Jada chirped. "We can find our way just fine."

"Okay, then" Gerald looked a bit disappointed. He looked as if he had something more to say but couldn't figure out how to say it. "You ladies have a wonderful evening."

"Thank you, Mr. Adams." I stated in my most demure voice. I felt kind of bad for rushing off once I saw how sad he looked. It was late and the last thing I needed was another love affair brewing. I was happy for the chance to forget about everything for an evening, but I had very real problems waiting for me once I got home. I didn't need to complicate my life any more by adding somebody new to the mix.

Jada had that gimme-the-dish look on her face when we got in the car. I knew I had some explaining to do.

"So?" Her brows raised like an excited little girl on Christmas morning who knows already that she has a bike.

"So what?" I was not going to make this easy for her.

"So you better tell me who the hell Al B. Sure was back there before I punch you in your eye!"

"Dang, girl!" I gave her my ghetto voice complete with smacks and all. "Why you always gotta be so violent?" We both laughed, but I knew I would still have to spill.

"Come on now, Mo. Quit playin'. He was on you from the time we walked in. Now what gives?"

"Aww, girl. You know better. All he was doing is talkin' and all I was doin' was lettin' him talk. He said his name was Gerald or something like that. He owns a few businesses in town. We really didn't say that much. I mostly drank the whole time."

"Mmm hmm. Well did Mr. Gerald or something like that happen to give you a last name? Or did you even ask while you were drinking?"

"I think it was Adams."

"Shamonica! Quit playin' with me!" She hit my arm hard.

"Ouch!" I frowned "Girl, what is the matter with you?"

"Mo, do you ever pay attention to *anything*?"

"I'm payin' attention to the fact that I'm about to smack you!"

"Mo, look up!" Jada was pointing to the marquee over the club which I had not seen until now. Written clearly in blue neon was '*The G.Q. Spot*'. I quickly pulled out the business card in my purse. Sure enough, there it was: 'Owner and operator – Gerald Quinton Adams.'

"Well I'll be damned." Suddenly embarrassment was an understatement for what I was feeling.

"Yeah, you need to be." Jada rolled her eyes. "Girl, only you could sit all night with the owner of a club all night on his birthday and not even give a damn. What am I going to do with you?"

"I don't know, but if you want him, you can have him. He probably wouldn't even know the difference if you called him anyway. There's no telling how many women he has pulled that mess on."

"Whatever, Mo'. All I know is there was only one woman he was pulling anything on tonight. Did you know he had security block off the fourth level? I finally just pushed passed the guy. The bouncer was on his way to stop me when I got to the table. I guess they were trying not to make a big scene, but you know me. I will clown when I have to." Now I understood why she had been so salty when Gerald suggested that Aaron walk us out.

"Jada, you are a mess. I'm so glad you're my friend. If you weren't, I'd have to have you committed." Jada let out an infectious laughter that had us in tears almost the whole way home.

None of what I found out really mattered to me.

Gerald almost became less attractive because of who he was. Who knew what his family was like or what kind of dreams they had for him and the type of woman he should be with. I knew just from this line of thinking that I should not call him. I needed time to dump some of this baggage. Who knew how long that would take?

When I got home, I tossed the business card in the side pocket of my briefcase along with a dozen others that I had gotten from potential clients or other networkers. Maybe I'd use it later, but probably not. Right then all I wanted to do was sleep.

Chapter Seven
Paula

Getting up Sunday morning was no easy task. Even though I slept in until eleven o'clock, I was still tired. That didn't matter. There was work to be done. I got up, took my shower, and was going to pull out all the information for my presentation as soon as I sobered up. I had another day without any distractions since I had sent the boys to Lena's the day before. I knew I had enough time to throw something together that would be halfway presentable. I just didn't know if I had the energy to do so. The presentation consisted of two ideas for a commercial, a few posters, and some information on the targeted demographic that my assistant had researched. We were trying to land an account with a rather large toy company. It seemed pretty cut and dry. The actual hard work had been put in months ago. This was just the icing on the cake, so to speak. I still had no plans to take this lightly.

In my years in this business, I've learned that sometimes the icing is what makes the cake.

I was on my way to the kitchen to get a cup of tea when I heard a frantic knock at my door. I was more startled at the break in silence than anything. I could see a thin silhouette through the opaque glass. I knew the figure was a woman with blonde hair, but I was perplexed at who it could be. She had an armful of what looked like books or maybe a box or something. I didn't think salespeople worked on Sundays. Even if they did, I was sure I didn't want whatever it was she would be pitching to me. I prepared my best 'no thanks' speech and opened the door.

"Ms. Peterson! Thank God I caught up with you." The frantic white woman at my door was my assistant. It wasn't unusual for her to stop by on occasion, but not unannounced.

"Paula, what are you –"

"Haven't you gotten any of my calls?"

She pushed passed me into the house and made a bee-line for the front den. This is where we normally got most of our work done. She had lots of folders in her hands and what looked like a couple of DVD's.

"Calls? When?"

I must've looked confused. I shook my head like a child protesting an angry parent. Then I realized how much of an affect my drinking the night before was having on me. My hand reflexively reached up to stop the bells from ringing in my ears. My eyes closed and opened again to try and refocus.

"Yes, calls. I tried to contact you all day yesterday and even left you a couple of messages. I wanted to talk to you about the Zimzam account. You aren't anywhere near ready to present this by tomorrow. I thought you might need these graphics that you left in your office. I found them Friday afternoon when you left work. I realized you must be trying to finish from home since you left early."

She took a brief pause and looked at me for what must've been the first time since she walked through the door.

"You don't look so well. Are you feeling okay, Ms. Peterson?"

"I'm fine, Paula. Can I offer you something to drink?"

"No, I'm fine. The sooner we can get started on this, the better I'll feel. I know how important deadlines are to you. I also know how hard we've worked on this. I do not intend for you to lose the account or your promotion because this is not ready by tomorrow."

"Well, then, I guess I'll go get my materials so we can get started."

It was like God had heard my silent prayer and answered it within minutes. I had just been thinking how much easier it would be if I had her to help me out. Paula was awesome. She always went above and beyond any expectations I had of her. I knew that this promotion meant a lot to her, as well. If I was promoted, there was a strong possibility that she would apply for my job. It had been rumored that my replacement would be an inside promotion rather than an outside hire. Paula knew that. She also knew more about my job than anyone else at that company. She probably knew more about this account than I did after having worked so closely with me for so long. Paula had a strong eye for details. If there was anything out of place, she would notice it and usually have a solution in mind before I had time to even give it a second glance. It was that talent that afforded her the ability to make strong work look even better. She never missed an opportunity to do so.

It didn't matter if she got my job or not, though. She had to know she would be well taken care of if she remained my assistant once I became a partner. It was a win/win situation for her. Even with this in mind, I figured she had only the purest of intentions for coming to my house to help me with this. I was still a bit on edge about her being there, though. There is just something I don't like about mixing my private life with life at the office. I was usually pretty good about keeping the two separate, but the entire week had been a mess. I was sure people were talking about me. Composure had not been a main focus for me that week. I was doing good just to show up each day. I knew Paula had seen how distracted I was. My wonder was if she would bring it up or not. All I could think about was trying to act like things were normal just long enough to get through this day. Then I would be able to breathe a lot easier.

All my materials were still sitting by the door in the laundry room where I had left them Friday afternoon. I came in from the garage that day feeling like I had just left a mental torture chamber. I dropped everything in a heap and started to go through the motions to make dinner and help Mathieu with his homework. Any other time I would have applauded him for his efforts to finish his homework on a Friday. Usually I had to end up fussing all night Sunday night before he would show any initiative to get it done. As Murphy's Law would have it, this time was different. By the time we were done with homework, he decided he wanted to go to my mother's for the weekend. She was always happy to have the boys come stay with her. Ever since my dad died, I suppose any company to take away from the silence of the empty house was a welcome break for her. Taking Mathieu to my mother's was a definite break for me, as well. Jacob would be coming to pick up Jackson the next day. I didn't know what was going to happen with that scenario. Looking back, I'm glad I had the forethought to not have him at the house. I only wish I had spared my youngest son from seeing what he saw. That's the thing with parenting. There are no second chances. You get one shot to raise an individual who is sane enough not to shoot everybody at his job just because he has a bad day. Yet, he must be just aggressive enough not to allow people to take advantage of him. It is a balancing act. Everything you do is an influence on who they will become. If you shelter them from everything, you are destined to have children who are uncertain or just plain apathetic about life. If you expose them to too much, they will develop some kind of social disorder. With boys it was even more crucial. I just hoped I hadn't failed either of my sons.

I gathered everything and prepared to move to the den. For a brief moment, it was like my feet couldn't move. My mind began to drift toward thoughts of Jacob and the insanity of what was actually about to happen tomorrow. I wondered if Salihah knew her father had bought me a washer and dryer. I laughed out loud at the childish nature of my question. Now I was being petty.

"Ms. Peterson!"

"I'm coming, Paula! I just have a few things in the garage, too! Give me a minute. Are you sure I can't offer you something to drink?" I lowered my voice as I entered the den again.

"Yes, I'm sure. Maybe I'll want something later, though. We are going to be here a while."

"Yeah, I know. Sorry to say it, but I haven't gotten much done this weekend, either. I was actually happy to see you. It's just been kind of crazy around here lately."

"Well!" She took a deep breath and stated in her chipper tone, "I'm here now, so let's get started." She knew something was awry. I could tell. I smiled to silently to thank her for not asking. She nodded to let me know that whatever it was I was going through was none of her concern.

"Yes," I chirped back "let's get started!"

Eight hours and two orders of take out later, we were done. That's the type of person Paula is. Once she has committed to a task, she is committed until it's finished. I loved the commercials she had brought with her. She also added some graphics to a slide presentation I had put together. I was sure the representatives from the toy company and my bosses were going to love the ideas we came up with. I was finally seeing all my months of work and research gel together. It always fascinates me. No matter how hard I work on something, seeing the finished presentation always makes me feel like I'm seeing the information for the first time. I wondered if Paula got the same rush I did from seeing a finished product like that.

She got up to leave and it became evident that my

mind was wandering again.

"Ms. Peterson…I…"

"Go ahead, Paula."

"Well, I hadn't wanted to say anything, but…"

"I know, Paula. I have been a bit distracted lately. I know you must be concerned."

"It's okay, Ms. Peterson, really. I understand. I mean everybody goes through our ups and downs. I just know how much this project means to you. I wouldn't want you to have to sacrifice your promotion for it not being completed."

"I feel the same way, Paula. It's just that I'm having trouble pushing past a very personal issue right now. I'm sure I'll do fine tomorrow."

"No offense, Ms. Peterson, but what makes you think that tomorrow will be any different than every day last week?"

I must've given a look that made her wish she could take back every word she had just said. Her discomfort was made obvious by her shifting from foot to foot. She could no longer look me in the eyes. I made a quick attempt to correct myself.

"Look, Paula, I don't want you to feel –"

"It's okay. I overstepped my boundaries. I understand. I do have one question, though."

"Go ahead."

"Would you have a problem with me doing the presentation?"

I stood in awe. Paula helping me with the project was one thing. I mean she had been an invaluable asset, but to have her be in a position to take credit for all my work was just preposterous. Once again she sensed my discomfort.

"Ms. Peterson, I have been working with you for over three years. I have never seen you like this. If I may be frank, I don't think you would be able to focus long enough to do the presentation tomorrow. Now I know that is a bold statement for me to make, and the last thing I would want to do is stand in your home and offend you. However, there are bigger things at stake here. We just spent eight hours working on this ad so that it would be ready to be pitched tomorrow. As I've heard you sometimes put it, Ms. Peterson, this icing is what is going to make this cake. If it isn't presented in an appealing way, they won't want to buy. All I'm asking is that you let me help you. I know almost as much as you do about the pitch. I paid attention to every detail we put together today from beginning to end. I have studied everything from the products themselves to the projected earnings that we can bring in with the commercials and other ads. I think if you give me a quick rundown of the final figures from the bobbly wobbly toy, I'll be set to go.

I'll even practice presenting it to you tonight. What do you have to lose?"

"Paula, you make some very good points. I'm almost convinced, but what will Mr. Kirkland and the other partners think. I mean, I was assigned to this and –"

"If your hesitation is that it will look like I'm trying to upstage you, please relax. I would never dream of taking credit for your work. I would be sure to make it very clear to Mr. Kirkland that you have the flu and that you send your deepest regrets that you could not appear in person. I mean they can't do anything about you being sick. Things just happen sometimes. You've already met the representatives from Zimzam Toys. They know how responsible you are. I'm just a fill in. I will make that very clear."

"The flu, huh?" I raised my eyebrow.

"The flu." She repeated with an intensity that let me know she was not going to change her story.

"Okay. I'm sold." I put my hands up in a stick-em-up position. "You got me. If your pitch for these ads is half that good, you'll have the account wrapped up before noon."

"Now, let's get me educated on this bobbly wobbly thing." She laughed.

"Paula," I was still a bit nervous.

"Yes."

"This is with the condition that you call me immediately after the presentation is over. If you have any problems at all, you have to call and let me know."

"You got it."

She smiled at me like a kid who was about to go on a field trip for the first time. This was a big responsibility, but we both knew she was more than qualified. The question was would the partners buy it or not. The Zimzam reps wouldn't know the difference. All they cared about was the bottom line - making money. We had that part covered. The partners of my company were another matter altogether. I didn't want them to think that I was ditching this assignment. It meant the world to me to even be chosen for the account. I hoped they wouldn't see this last minute change as a slap in the face.

Once I was sure Paula knew everything she needed to know, I began to get more comfortable with the thought of her pitching my ideas. There was still that nagging feeling that she might steal the credit for them, though. I mean I wouldn't have even blamed her if she thought about it. She had contributed a lot of useful information for me. Maybe she would feel like she was owed that credit. Only time would tell. I couldn't dwell on my decision. I just made up my mind that whatever happened, I would be okay with it. I don't think a greater lie had ever been told. All I knew was that she was right about me not being able to make the presentation myself.

I decided to call my children, catch the late show, and call it a night. The worries of Monday would have to take care of themselves.

Chapter Eight
Jacob

"Come on, man, this is supposed to be your bachelor party. Lighten up. You're sittin' here lookin' like you're going to your funeral tomorrow instead of your wedding."

"I am." Jacob took another shot of the top shelf tequila he'd been knocking back all night.

"Look man. If it's that bad, why don't you just back out now and go back to Mo'?"

"Don't you think I would if I could?"

Jacob couldn't tell if it was the liquor that had him so fired up or if Marcus' comment was just that stupid. Either way, he wanted to hit something...or someone. It was clear that he needed a bit of fresh air.

Outside it was evident that nightlife was in full effect. Women were whizzing by in their party clothes. Men were driving by slowly to watch them. Each one stared the other down to find out if this could be the love connection they had waited for all night. The games were all in action as female vs. male continued up and down the strip.

Jacob and his friends were downtown having his bachelor party at one of the most expensive nightclubs in the city. This was one of the many amenities that Jacob could now afford since his soon to be father-in-law had basically opened up the family bank account to him. The atmosphere inside was great. There were plenty of beautiful women, and lots of good liquor. There was only one thing on Jacob's mind …Shamonica. He wished so badly to be able to totally erase the last four months of his life. He wanted to go back and somehow undo all the wrong he had gotten himself into. He knew that there would be no way to make her see his side of this. That was why he had been so short with her just five nights earlier.

"Hey, man! The party is inside. What you doin' out here?" Jacob stared blankly into the darkness as if he hadn't heard a word.

"Marcus, you remember the day I met Shamonica?"

"Yeah I remember. Every guy at that party wanted to talk to her. I remember she was lookin' at me and yo' player hatin' ass stepped in." They shared a small laugh.

"Man, next to the day Jackson was born, that was the happiest day of my life! I remember thinking that I had finally found my queen. I had to do whatever it took to keep her happy. I didn't care what sacrifices I had to make. She was my number one priority, and it all started that day. From the very first moment I saw her."

"Yeah, I know. Some of her happiness was even at my expense. By the way, you never did pay me back that $50 I loaned you the night y'all went to the Jill Scott Concert."

Jacob knew Marcus was trying to lighten the mood, but he felt anything but light. His heart was heavy with guilt and embarrassment over how he had treated the woman whom he claimed to love.

"Marcus, I'm serious, man. It's like this shit is a deep black hole just sucking me in. I shouldn't be here tonight about to marry anybody but Mo'. I just wish there was some kinda way out of this."

"Look, if you really feel that way, then don't go through with it. There is the slim possibility that she'll take you back. All I know is that once you walk down that aisle, it's over. Curtains down, lights out...over. Man, I'll be honest with you. I've never seen you the way you are when you're with Mo'. It's obvious how you two feel about each other. But you gotta look at the damage that's been done. You chose a hell of a way to tell her about all of this. You *said* you wanted to do it this way so that there would be less drama and no emotional outbursts on her part. I think you did it so you would have to go through with the wedding no matter what. Man, Mo' may love you, but I don't know *any* woman that could stay with a man after all this. You knew that when you decided to marry this girl. Whatever the case may be, Jacob, you made the situation what it is. All I'm telling you to do is think before you make it any worse. Eventually you are going to have to stick with a decision. Even if it happens to be a bad one."

"You're right. I just can't wrap my mind around spending my life with anybody other than her. I mean she has stuck with me through a lot, man. You know how I was before I met her. I have never been with a woman like Mo'. She has changed my life for the better. Now I'm about to end up with somebody who I don't even love because of a stupid mistake."

"I'm not gonna stand here and tell you I know what you're going through. I don't want to come down on you like some kind of judge, either. All I know is that you guys had a great thing going and it surprised the hell out of us all when you decided to bail out all of a sudden. I understood when you said you were trying to improve your money situation and all, but you would think the chick was pregnant or something the way you just up and decided to get hitched!" Jacob never moved. His expression said everything without him having to say a word. He put his head down and allowed Marcus to come to the very obvious conclusion.

"Look, man, this wasn't supposed to happen like this. It was just supposed to be a quick courtship and then I was going to send her back home. I would get a little cash, she would get to see the U.S., and both our parents would get off our backs about the marriage thing."

"I guess baby girl's game is tighter than yours, huh?"

"What! Man, please!"

"Naw, Jacob. Think about it. She played the player. You said yourself that she loved being here and that your mom has treated her like a part of the family since day one. Why would she want to go back home? Especially with her knowing that you're a legal citizen. That baby and this marriage have assured her the right to stay here for life! You fell for that little wide-eyed innocent act, too. Don't tell me you didn't. She played you like B.B. plays Lucille, man. She didn't hold back nothin'!"

"You got it all wrong, man. Salihah didn't even want this. She was upset when she found out about the baby. That was one of the reasons I told her I would marry her rather than see her be disowned. Her father is a very proud man. He would kill us both if he knew."

"Well how upset was she the night the baby was conceived? Come on, man. You can't tell me you don't see this. You told me that you never even planned to have sex with her. Think about how it went down, man. You have done some dumb shit in your time, but you should've seen this comin'."

Jacob began to think of the situation in a totally different way now. Maybe he had been played. Salihah had seduced him just one month after her arrival. He was upset over a fight he had with Shamonica, and went to his mother's that night to get away. He didn't tell anyone he was there, and even went to the trouble of taking the back entranceway in. Jacob was half asleep in the back guest room when Salihah walked in. She had on a rather skimpy nightgown. She told him she had just come in to look for a pair of slippers she thought she had left in there. It never hit him until now that she must've seen his truck in the garage. He usually parked on the street. They talked for a while about what was bothering him. She had to know he was drunk and not thinking clearly. Before long they were kissing. The cheap liquor and hormones took over from there.

Jacob decided the next morning that Salihah had to go. He felt guilty about cheating on Shamonica and was determined that it would never happen again. He devised a plan to have Salihah back to Africa in eight weeks. Just long enough for him to get the money he needed to pay off the debt incurred from opening his shop. Jacob felt indebted to Shamonica, too. She had sacrificed a lot to help him open his business. He was determined to show her that the investment was paying off. She had been very understanding when he told her that business had been slow. He knew that understanding would eventually run out. Jacob needed to show her results. Now that they were living together, it was even more crucial. He was expected to be the head of his household. Jacob would never get to prove himself.

Six weeks after the night they slept together, Jacob found out Salihah was pregnant. It was now clear why she had been against an abortion. In Jacob's mind, that would've solved everything. He even offered to stay with her during the entire procedure. Salihah said that she couldn't fathom the thought of killing her own flesh and blood. At the time Jacob thought it was because of her morals and her traditional upbringing. Now he was seeing more clearly.

Maybe this was just karma paying him back for all the times he had scammed people. All he knew was that he was about to give up on the best thing that had ever happened to him. Marcus was right. The wheels had already been set into motion. To back out now would mean that Salihah's father would find out about everything. For his own safety, Jacob couldn't let that happen. He decided to go home and get some rest before the next day's sentencing.

"Look, Marcus, I got a lot on my mind right now. I need to go. You guys enjoy the party. I'll see you tomorrow."

"Sure thing, man. Look, I hope I wasn't out of line."

"I'm fine. You gotta call 'em like you see 'em. I mean, hey, what do I have to worry about? I'm getting' married tomorrow, right?"

"Yeah. Well, just don't do anything crazy before then. If you need me to drive you home –"

"Man, look. I said I'm fine. I'll see you tomorrow. You just be sure to catch that tab tonight."

"Yeah, right! Now I know you've been drinkin' too much!"

On the way back to his mother's, Jacob passed by the house he used to call home. This was out of the way for him, but he just felt like he needed to pass by. He hadn't expected to pay Shamonica a visit. There was nothing to say. He just wanted to feel like he was near her. Surprisingly, a small light was on in the living room. The flicker of the television beat against the far wall of the room. Jacob decided that maybe this was his chance to explain to her what had been going on. He parked his truck on the street in front of the house and approached the walkway. If she was awake, maybe she was thinking about him, too. Maybe she would be able to hear and understand all that went wrong over the last few months. Maybe this was just the tequila giving him false hope.

Jacob stopped halfway up the walkway. Through the

sheer curtains of the front room he could see Shamonica sleeping on the couch. She looked like an angel. As far as Jacob was concerned, she was his angel. Only this time she would not be able to rescue him from himself like she had done before. This time he would have to face the situation head on and hope for the best. He trudged back down the walkway, started up the Chevy, and prepared to return home where he would sleep away his last hours of freedom.

By the time he got to his mother's house, everyone was already asleep. Jacob grabbed a blanket and a pillow and decided to retire on the sofa. He drifted off immediately holding the pillow in his arms, and thinking of how peaceful Shamonica had looked. In his dream, they were together. Jacob slept better than he had in months.

Chapter Nine
Monday Morning

I had fallen asleep on the couch Sunday night watching the late show. My neck was a bit stiff, and my joints felt like the Tin Man must feel when he needs oiling. I called in for work and took my shower. Lena assured me that the boys had made it off to school okay, and then it occurred to me that I didn't have anything to do all day. I hadn't had that feeling in months. I had no idea what to do with myself. I knew I couldn't just sit around the house, so I decided to go see my mother.

My mother's house is a typical little grandmotherly cottage. I could see why my children liked it there so much. She always had enticing aromas coming from her kitchen no matter what time of day it was. Although no one was living there but her, you would swear she had an army to feed. The aroma de jour was gingerbread this morning. I could smell it from the driveway, and the fragrance just got more irresistible as I got closer to the door. It was still early, and I could hear her gospel music playing. She had opened the front door and was allowing the screen door to filter the wonderful smells from her kitchen out to the neighborhood. I doubt that she had any worries about crime. Everyone loved my mother. I sometimes worried about her trusting nature. She would always tell me she had nothing to worry about as long as the Father, Son, and Holy Ghost had her back. (She had learned new slang terms from Mathieu and never hesitated to use them.) That was my mama. I don't believe I have ever seen her worry about anything. She seemed to change effortlessly with the times and never had any regrets about the past. She was a wonderful example. I just never felt like I could live up to that high of a standard.

"Mama!" I knocked on the side of the screen door.

"Yes, child! Come on in! It's open!" She was still in the kitchen. I wiped my feet on the mat and proceeded toward the heavenly scents of what must have been her sanctuary for years.

"Mama, you really shouldn't leave the door open like that."

"And good morning to you, too, Shamonica." She gave me that I-know-I-raised-you-better-than-that look.

"I'm for real, Mama." I attempted to make my point appear more important than hers. I don't know why I even bothered. A good mama look trumps all.

"I'm for real, too. Now that door swings both ways. You go get on the other side of it until you think you can enter my home properly."

"I'm sorry. Good morning, Mama." I gave her a big hug and a kiss. I don't know if it was more for her benefit or mine, but I was starting to feel better just being in her presence.

"Now that's my Pumpkin. Can I get you some breakfast, Baby?"

Mama had eggs, grits, sausage, and pancake mix all ready to be thrown on the stove. There was no such thing as a light breakfast in this house. The hungry would not leave the way they came. I believe that was how she put it. I laughed at the sight of all that food. I hadn't eaten a full breakfast in what seemed like ages.

"Yes, ma'am, you can. I feel like I haven't eaten in days."

"Well that's what heartache can do to you, baby."

My mother never minced words. If she wanted to know something or wanted you to know she knew something, she just would say it. I like that about her, but today when I was trying to escape everything, it just didn't feel quite right. I felt like the wind had been knocked out of me again. My smile faded quickly.

"So Lena told you, huh?"

"No, Lena didn't tell me anything. Jacob came by here Saturday. I guess he figured you would bring Jackson here after everything that happened at the house."

"How much did he tell you?"

"He told me enough to let me know that you were both wrong." I couldn't believe my ears. Whose side was she on?

"Who me?"

"Yes, *you*! Unless you're going to tell me you didn't really chase him out of your driveway yelling and cursing. You don't ever let anyone push you to the point of acting like that, Baby. You stand strong and be the woman you are at all times. I don't care if he brought his fiancée, his mama, and their dog, too. Shamonica has to be Shamonica. Baby, I'm not fussin'. I know you were acting out of emotion. Jacob was flat out wrong for how he handled this thing. Don't think I didn't tell him about himself, too. But, Baby, you are *my* daughter. I care about what happens to *you*. I know you have children that you have to answer to. Those boys need you to be strong. Sometimes men can do some foolish stuff. You just remember that you have to conduct yourself in a way that allows you to still call yourself a lady at the end of the day."

I don't think I was ready for that strong a dose of truth. I guess I expected her to just understand my point of view and not take anything else into consideration. That was not the way my mother operated. She just wasn't built that way. She insisted on having both sides of a story. Even then, she wouldn't choose. She just stated truth and let that stand.

"Well, what was I supposed to do, Mama? Jacob disrespected my household and everyone in it by even bringing that woman on my side of town let alone in my driveway."

"You did what I would expect any young woman in your same position to do, Shamonica. You made it very clear to him that neither he nor his 'fiancée' were welcome in or at your home. All I'm saying is that there is always a choice, Baby. Think before you act. Jackson didn't need to see everything that he saw." She took a deep breath. "But! There's no use dwelling on all that. What's done is done. What I want to know is what are you going to do now?"

"That's what I wanna know, too, Mama."

I sat on the high barstool in her kitchen and allowed my feet to swing back and forth. I felt like I was twelve years old again and was talking to my mama about the bullies at school who would tease me. I never felt like there was a way out back then, but Mama always had an answer for everything.

"Well, Baby, Mama can't tell you what to do, but I'll certainly be here to listen to you and feed ya while you get it all figured out." She pinched my cheek and gave me another hug. I wanted to stay in her arms forever. She was so strong and so loving all at the same time.

"Mama?"

"What's up, Baby Girl?" She turned to check her gingerbread cookies. I was sure they were done.

"Did Jacob say anything else?"

"Naw, Baby Girl. You know he didn't want to tarry long once I had my say about him getting married. I didn't want to judge him, but there is a right and a wrong way to do things. The way he is going about all this is all wrong. You can't just walk away from a person the way he's doing and expect anything but heartache and trouble to follow you. Now you know I don't take sides. Fact of the matter is that I'd rather stay out of your business altogether. I just had to let him know that I didn't appreciate how he was disrespecting our family. We have done a lot for that boy. He and your daddy had a good relationship before he passed. Johnny would be turnin' over in his grave if he could see this right now." She let out an exasperated sigh.

"Am I wrong to want him back, Mama?"

"Wrong? Child, that's just down right natural! The man *broke* your heart. He didn't take away your ability to love altogether. You two have a history together. While the time spent together wasn't as long as your father and me, you still had a soul tie to the man. You can't just get rid of that because one or the other decides to move on. Make no mistake about it, Honey. That boy is miserable. I have prayed for you both ever since I found out what was going on. It's gonna take some time, Baby Girl, but

I know you'll make it through this. Nobody can tell you where to go or how to get there, though. This is going to be your own journey. I know it doesn't feel like it right now, Shamonica, but you are strong enough to handle this. I know The Father would never put anything on you that you weren't strong enough to bear. You are going to come through as pure gold, Child."

"I just wish he would talk to me. He's treating me like *I* did something wrong. Like it's my fault the relationship is ending. I was hit over the head with this thing like a sack of bricks. No discussion. No compassion. Just 'bye'. He didn't even have the decency to tell me in the privacy of our own home. He took me out to dinner like he had good news for me or something! Then he just sprung the news on me! He said was getting married, and that his fiancée was pregnant. Then, come to find out, the wedding is today! He just told me about all this on Tuesday, Mama!"

I was getting upset now. I hadn't really shared my feelings with anybody other than Mary Poppins when I went to see her on Saturday. This hurt, but at least I knew my mama was actually listening to me. I finally had a chance to get it out. My announcement about him not talking this over with me was news to my mother. From the look on her face when I said the word 'pregnant', I knew she didn't know about that either. I could tell she was now angry. She wasn't like me, though. She chose to keep quiet in times like this until she could think of exactly what she needed to say. She really adhered to the rule that if you couldn't say something nice, you should remain silent.

"Lord, Lord! Help us Father! I know you're a way maker, God. This family needs you right now."

My mother had no problems praying out loud. She did this quite often when she knew there was a delicate situation at hand. 'Why talk to the problem,' she would say. 'I talk to The Master. He can fix it all, and we can't.' I knew she was right, but somehow right now I didn't feel like I could get a prayer past the ceiling. I had so much anger and other things going on inside me that I doubted if The Father would even be able to hear past the screams and cursing of my broken spirit.

"Shamonica, have you had a chance to talk to the boys about what's going on?"

"Well, I told Jackson Saturday morning that his father was getting married. He asked if Jacob was marrying me and I had to say no. I don't have any answers for him past that. Jacob hasn't even given me any answers. I'm not going to tell the boys about the baby. I feel like Jacob should have to be the one to do that. He has put me through enough. The least he can do is accept responsibility for breaking the news to these children. They idolize him."

"Amen to that!"

"Mama, I owe you an apology."

"For what, baby?"

"You told me when Jacob and I were about to move in together that I should get married first. You always said that there was an order to things. If I followed the order, I would be blessed. If I tried to step ahead, I was just looking for trouble. I guess if I had listened to you I wouldn't be in the situation I'm in now."

"Shamonica, you don't owe me anything, Child. Your life and all the choices that go with it belong to you. As long as you have taken the time to make things right with God, what I think doesn't matter one bit. And anyway, do you think it would hurt you any less if y'all weren't living together? Baby, people do what they do in life for the strangest reasons. We have no control over that. The only person you have control over on this earth is you. Jacob made up in his mind that this was what he wanted. Him not having a key to your residence wouldn't have made a lick of difference."

"I guess you're right, but at least I'd be getting half of the business if we had been married."

"And that was going to make you feel better? Having the rights to a rundown shack of a garage with three lazy employees and a miserable owner? Was that going to do it for you?" She chuckled.

I had never heard my mother talk like that about Jacob's garage. She had always encouraged him to keep trying to make it the business he had dreamed of. I knew she was letting out some of that bitterness now. I'll admit, it almost made me feel better. Just knowing that she was a little more human. A little more like me.

"No, ma'am, I guess it wouldn't. I just wish... Oh, I don't know!"

My frustration was taking over. I was really upset now. I just wanted to wrap myself into a little ball and hide until all this blew over. This was reality. There was no good hiding place from that.

"Shamonica," My mother once again put her arms around me. "I love you child. God loves you, and I love you. When this gets harder, and it will get harder, you just remember that. My door is always open, Baby."

My mother held me like her life depended on this one embrace. Maybe it was my life that depended on it. I didn't know. I just knew I was tired. It was like that was all I could feel then. We hugged for a while and talked some more. I ate breakfast and prepared to go home. I wanted to stay longer, but I also wanted to be alone. The latter desire won out. My mother made sure to pack some gingerbread men for the boys. I was sure they would never see them. My plan was to go home and wrap up in front of the TV with a big bowl of applesauce and scarf them down while I watched cartoons. It was like she read my mind.

"Now those are for my babies, 'Mo. You make sure they get *some* of them."

"Okay, Mama." I lied.

On my way home, I thought a lot about my father. He was not as spiritual as my mother and definitely had a different way of handling things. I laughed at the thought of what he would be saying right now. I had no doubt he would've pulled out that rusty shotgun of his and declared to the world that, "That boy is dead!" I didn't have my dad anymore. There was no one to kiss me on the forehead and tell me not to worry because they had it all taken care of. I loved my father and missed him every day. Especially this day, though, his memory was so strong that he was almost tangible.

I couldn't help but think about the rape now. That was the hardest thing I had ever been through. I remembered my dad and how frustrated he used to look during that period of our lives. It was like he was lost. He wanted so badly to make everything better, but he didn't know how. Our relationship changed a lot during that time. We talked very little before I had Mathieu. I thought it was because he was ashamed of me. I didn't find out until later just how overwhelming this whole thing was for him. He had actually hired a private detective to try to find the guy who did it. Of course, he told me nothing about it. When my mother found out, she told him to fire the guy. My mother knew my father all too well. He told her that he wanted the rapist found and brought to justice. She knew that 'justice' didn't necessarily mean the county holding cell. I still don't know if he ever found him or not. No arrests were ever made in my case. If anything ever came of the situation, my father took that to the grave with him. Our relationship improved after Mathieu was born. It was like my son had given us all a new perspective on things. He was the most important thing to us all. The hurt and pain didn't exist anymore. All any of us could feel was love for this tiny precious gift that had been given to us. I never explained to Mathieu the circumstances surrounding his conception. I always thought if he asked I would tell him when he was old enough. I hated Jacob for giving me, yet another, hard truth that I would have to break to my son.

Chapter Ten
The Wedding Day

When I came from my mother's I retired in the same spot I had been in the night before. I knew I would probably fall asleep, so I made sure I was prepared. My alarm clock was set for 4:30P.M. I didn't want to forget to call Paula to see how the presentation had gone. I knew she was supposed to call me, but I didn't want to take any chances. I remember waking up at exactly 2:15 P.M. I looked at the clock on the wall and thought to myself that she should have been finishing up by then. I don't know why, but all of a sudden I started crying uncontrollably. I felt so bad that I was barely able to drag myself upstairs to my bedroom. Lena showed up a few hours later to check on me. She had taken the boys to my mother's house when she picked them up from school. I was still in the same heap in the middle of my bed when she got there.

"Mo', you don't look good! How many of these did

you take?" Lena picked up the bottle on my bedside table. "Do I need to call Dr. Ross? Mo', talk to me!"

Lena was a nurse practitioner. She could write prescriptions for her patients, but never wrote them for her family because of the conflict of interest. In this case, she had made a bit of an exception. She had talked to the physician she works with and got her to write me a prescription for some Xanax to help me cope with everything. They were supposed to be pills to decrease anxiety. I had taken one of them when I came upstairs because I figured I was having another anxiety attack.

"I only took one, Lena. Don't worry. If I was gonna kill myself, I'd at least get my hair done first."

I gave a dry chuckle at my own attempt at humor. Lena wasn't laughing. She was almost crying. She hopped onto the bed and grabbed me in her arms.

"Come on, Sis! You have to get through this! I can't watch you like this anymore, Mo'! I don't know what to do! It's like you just go into your own little cave and try to shut the rest of us out! Show me how to help you!"

Lena was sobbing now. I think this was probably the second time I've ever seen my sister cry as an adult. The first was when my father died. She was normally tower of strength and wisdom. She was the older, smarter sister. I had always been able to lean on her. It was very strange to see her breaking like this.

"I'm sorry, Lena." I buried my head in the pillow I was holding.

"Mo', there's nothing to be sorry about. You didn't cause all of this. Jacob did. All I want to know is how to help you get through it. I have patients everyday with problems that I can fix. Give a pill for this, an ointment for that. Mo', they didn't teach me how to fix broken hearts. I don't know what to do. I see you hurting and all I can do is hurt, too."

"Just being here is enough, Lena. I don't know how to do this. I don't know if there's a right way to be thrown away. If you find one, let me know. Every hope that I had for the future was buried in this family. I feel lost without him, Lena. He was to me what Daddy was to Momma. I know that's hard for you to believe, but that's what it was. Now that I don't have that anymore I guess I have to completely shut down and reboot."

"Well, I'll be here for you whenever you need, Sis. I'm just really scared for you. It's like I'm watching you self-destruct. You don't know what that does to me. I mean, you may have loved Jacob, but no man is worth all this."

"Lena, if I could decide how to feel, I would. Do you think I want to feel like this? Not knowing when I'm just gonna spontaneously turn into a damn water fountain! I'm tired of crying! I'm tired of not being able to think straight. I'm tired of going over all our videos and photo albums wondering when it was that he started plotting all this. Was it when Jackson was born? Maybe last year's family reunion, Lena. No! Maybe it was at daddy's funeral. Or maybe it was three years ago at Uncle Jeff's wedding. Girl, you don't have any idea about what I'm going through. You have a good husband, Lena. You have somebody who loves you and comes home to *you* at night. Am I wrong for missing that feeling? Am I wrong to want the same thing?"

Lena took a deep breath and let out an exasperated sigh. I knew I had crossed the line with that last comment. Lena and her husband had been through a lot. They had really just gotten things back together over the last two years or so. He started working offshore and things got a lot better. He was gone just enough for her to miss him, but at home enough to raise his family and be there for them when they needed him. They had discussed divorce a couple of times, but always decided that their relationship was worth saving. She did have a good marriage, but it had come over time.

"Mo', I'm not gonna tell you how to live your life. All I want to do is help you make it through this."

"Thank you, Lena."

"Look, Mama is making dinner tonight and wants all of us to be there. I think it would do you some good to be around everybody. Brock is home for two weeks, and we're bringing the kids. You know you haven't seen your nieces in over a week. You owe it to the girls to be there. You know how much they love their Auntie MoMo. Besides, the boys have terrorized them this weekend. You know Brook can't wait to tell you all about it. Bailey has already made out an itemized list of things from her room she wants you to replace."

"I'll be there, Lena. Just give me some time to straighten up the house. I know Mathieu probably left his room a mess. I was planning to try and clean over the weekend while they were gone. I just haven't had the energy." I started to cry again. Lena still held me. "Lena, you think he really went through with it?"

She took a long pause before speaking. It was the kind of pause people take when they have something grim to tell someone.

"Yeah, Mo', he did. I spoke with Naji before I came by. The wedding was at two o'clock. It was fairly short. The ceremony was at his mother's house. Naji said it was over before three."

I felt that tingling feeling again in my hands. My head began to spin with all the thoughts of things Jacob had told me over the years. Suddenly, nothing he ever said held meaning anymore. All the loving words and gestures just seemed pointless. I drifted off as the medicine began to take its effect. Lena continued to try to encourage me. She said that he had been crazy from day one and that I was better off without him. My ears processed the sounds to my brain, but somehow my heart missed the message.

$$\boldsymbol{\omega}$$

Jacob looked in the mirror one last time as he prepared to enter his mother's backyard. This was the day that he would finally follow through with something. He had tossed and turned for weeks thinking about this day. He laughed at himself over the irony of the only comfort he had the night before. Thoughts of Shamonica had lulled him into a deep sleep where he remained until the harsh reality of morning crashed through the curtains of his mother's living room the next morning. Now here he stood about to walk down the aisle with a woman who, until a few short months ago, he didn't even know.

"Jacob, you are a real jackass." He shook his head at his reflection.

"You can say that again." Marcus put his hand on his best friend's shoulder.

"So now you're eavesdropping?"

"Oh, my bad, did you two want to be alone?"

"You know, if that accounting thing doesn't work out for you, you might want to look into something else. Just don't do comedy!"

"Well, good for me, accounting is looking good. Back

to you, though, are you ready, man?"

"I may as well be. It looks like it's going to happen."

"Man, look, nobody would blame you if you…"

"Let's go, Marcus. They're waiting."

Jacob knew what Marcus was about to suggest. Running was not an option. He had to follow this thing through. He knew Marcus had been right about one thing. He was going to have to stick with a decision. Albeit a seemingly bad decision, the choice had been made. It was now time to make it official. The small crowd was mostly made up of a few of Jacob's friends and his employees with their families. Many of Jacob's family members didn't even show up. This was a bit of a silent protest for some. For others it was just a result of the short notice of the event. He only had his brother and his best friend to stand for him. Had it not been for his mother, Jacob was sure Naji would not have come, either. He decided not to bring Jackson because he didn't want to fight with Shamonica anymore. Besides that, he didn't want to make his son attend a wedding that never should have been happening in the first place. He felt guilty enough for having to explain to Jackson that he was marrying someone other than his mother. There was no way to justify making him watch as it happened.

As for Salihah's family, they would all be present for the big party her father was throwing the next month in Nigeria. Her sister lived in the U.S., and flew in to stand witness to today's event. It had been decided that a traditional ceremony would be held after the American one.

Jacob strolled down the aisle trying not to allow his dissatisfaction with himself to show on his face. He glanced at his watch when he reached the minister. It was two fifteen. He couldn't help but wonder what Shamonica was doing. He wondered if her presentation had gone okay. If there was ever a time that he would run, this would have been it. He shoved his hands deep into his pockets as if to weigh himself down. Just then, Salihah appeared at the threshold of the doorway. She began to slowly approach him, and Jacob knew this was the end.

Chapter Eleven
The Promotion

I was still half asleep, but I heard the phone ring. Lena was in the process of telling the caller that I was not available when I got up. I figured it must be Paula. I picked up the phone on my nightstand.

"Hello! Paula?"

"Yes, Ms. Peterson I have good news!"

"The presentation went well, then?"

I was beginning to wake up. This was just the good news I needed to hear to bring me out of this rut. All my hard work was about to pay off. At least if my personal life was in shambles, I had something good going for me.

"Not just good! Even better!" She was beginning to sound like a chipper cheerleader.

"Okay, Paula, spit it out!" I couldn't hide my anxiety. My whole life was hanging in the balance, and she was making me pry this out of her.

"Well, first of all, they loved the presentation. Mr. Kirkland like it so much that he gave me your office!"

I saw red. I couldn't believe what I was hearing. Had my worst fear come to pass? This woman had weaseled me out of my job *and* my promotion all in one day!

"He what?" I couldn't hide my anger and my voice began to get louder.

"Well, yeah, he gave me your office." She paused. "I guess he didn't think you'd need it since he moved you upstairs to the corner office of the executive floor."

I jumped out of bed and knocked over the glass on my nightstand in my excitement.

"Oh, my God! Paula, did I just hear you say what I thought you said?"

"Yes, ma'am! You got the promotion!"

"Oh, my God.... Oh, my God!"

I couldn't stop jumping. Now Paula and I both sounded like cheerleaders. I was in the middle of my wild happy dance when Lena came in.

"I guess you're cured, huh?"

She was a bit confused. She had no idea who was on the phone. I guess I picked up before they got a chance to exchange that information.

"Lena! I got the promotion!"

Lena knew what this meant to me, so she was excited as well. She's never been the cheerleader type. She congratulated me and began to gather her things.

"That is so wonderful, Mo'! Look, I'm gonna go get Brock and the girls ready to head over to Mama's. I'll let you tell everybody the good news when you get there tonight." She gave me a quick kiss and a hug and was gone.

"*Hello…helloooo?*"

I had forgotten Paula was on the phone.

"Oh! Paula, I'm so sorry!"

"It's okay. I understand you're excited. I am, too. I didn't finish telling you everything. The first assignment has already been made out for you."

"Well, what is it?"

"They want you to research a new company that has asked us to handle their advertising. Are you familiar with Sundown Resorts?"

"Well, yeah! They have great resorts all over the U.S. What do they need me for? They seem to have a great ad campaign going."

"They aren't advertising for existing resorts. They just opened a new one in Puerto Rico. It will be our job to research the resort and come up with ads to attract new customers."

"Okay, I'll get right on it. Did they send any information about the place?"

"Well, that's the thing. Mr. Kirkland figured it would be best to gather information firsthand, so he's sending us there to see the new resort."

I couldn't believe my ears.

"Paula, are you serious?"

"Very. I guess he figures the trip will do you some good. When you get back from your sick leave that is. He said you hadn't looked like yourself lately. He wasn't even surprised when I told him you had the flu."

All the paperwork had been filed for my promotion already. Mr. Kirkland never had any intentions on giving that position to anyone else. Paula had gone to see my new office out of curiosity. Maintenance had already put my name on the door. All I had to do was go by Human Resources and sign a few forms. The trip had been taken care of as well. She went on to tell me that we would be leaving in about a week and a half. Paula was going to come with me. I was basically supervising her work now. She would be in charge of putting together the ad. I was the liaison between our agency and the representative from the resort. This was a big step for us both. I must say I was glad to have her working with me. I don't think I would have been as comfortable with anyone else.

I quickly composed myself and prepared to go back to my mother's house. I tried hard to focus on the promotion. I still had this nagging feeling about the whole thing with Jacob, but I was determined not to let it ruin this for me. I couldn't let my family see me in the state I had been in before Lena walked in. I showered and changed in record time. I couldn't wait to see my sons. I had talked to them over the phone, but Mathieu had been gone since Friday and Jackson since Saturday. I wanted to hug them both to pieces. They were my real family. I needed to be strong now for them. It was time to come out of mourning.

As I made my way down the stairs, I took in the full view of my home making mental notes of everything that needed to be remodeled. There were pictures that would be taken down, and furniture to be moved out. I made up my mind to use the rest of the week to do those things. Paula told Mr. Kirkland that I would be out for the rest of the week. I saw no reason to make her out to be a liar. I would have plenty of time to prepare for the trip the next week. I fully trusted Paula to clean out my old office and move my stuff into the new one. Things at work would just have to wait. I had to take care of home.

I made it to my mother's house just in time for dinner. I think Lena probably made everyone wait until I got there. My nieces were overjoyed to see me. They always were. As happy as I was to see them, I had two other very special people in mind.

"Mom-meeeee!" Jackson yelled as he raced to be the first to jump into my arms.

"Hey, mom!" Mathieu was trying to play it cool. The older he got, the less he liked hugs and kisses. I guess he is a typical boy. He hugged me anyway. Partially to satisfy me, but I knew he really missed me.

"Hello, my handsome men! I have missed you two very very much!" I squeezed them together like a son sandwich. I was pretty sure I heard one of them gasping for air, so I let go.

"Girl, you're gonna squeeze the life out of those kids! Let 'em go and come hug somebody more your size!" My brother-in-law Brock was nowhere near my size. He was a tall muscular man with arms big enough to crush me.

"When you see somebody *my* size, you let me know!" We shared a laugh and a friendly hug.

I proceeded to the dining room where the table had already been set. Lena and my mother were bringing out the food. The spread was huge. We all sat down and Brock blessed the meal. I said my own silent prayer to thank God for allowing me to be around my family like this. It seemed like just what I needed to change my perspective. The food was great and the company was even better. Everyone was thrilled to hear about my promotion. Brook and Bailey had stars in their eyes thinking about all the extra gifts they would be getting with my raise. Lena and I had made a habit of spoiling one another's children. It was fairly easy since she had girls and I had boys. There was very little jealousy among the cousins. Their ages were spread out enough to control jealousy between siblings as well. Brook and Bailey were twelve and nine. Mathieu and Jackson were eight and four. The only problems we had were the normal sibling rivalry issues. This one complaining about that one "getting away with murder" from time to time. All in all, we had a pretty happy family. I felt proud as I looked around the table at the people who loved me. I remember thinking how lucky I was just to be able to have this many people in my life who truly cared about me. I still felt the void. It was hard not to notice that Jacob wasn't there. I had to come to the conclusion that this was going to be the way things were. Maybe he was right. Maybe I just needed to deal with it.

Chapter Twelve
Taking Back the House

Jada was already waiting for me Tuesday morning when I got home from taking the boys to school. I had called her the night before to ask for help rearranging the house. If nothing else could be said for Jada, she was always there in a pinch. Especially today, she was all too eager to help me get the last traces of Jacob out of my life...well, out of my house, anyway.

"Hey, girl! Where you wanna start? You wanna burn his clothes or his pictures first?"

She was trying to be funny, but I saw a hint of seriousness in those eyes of hers.

"It's not even that type of party, girl. Besides, Jacob took most of his stuff when he left. Whatever's here is just stuff that either he didn't want, or things that belonged to us both. I just want to take down all the pictures and give the house a new feel."

"Okay, then. Let's get to project 'Bachelorette Pad'!"

"Jada, you are a hot mess!"

"And you love me for it!"

"Yes I do, Girl. Yes I do."

We started in the bedroom since that's my sanctuary. My bedroom was the last place I wanted any traces of Jacob. It was hard enough sleeping alone. I certainly didn't want to have to look at pictures of him everywhere when I woke up. I wanted to hang some new pictures and a painting I had bought months earlier. I had no idea where to put it when I bought it. I was happy the investment was going to pay off. I also wanted to rearrange my furniture. That was no easy task. I never realized how heavy my bedroom furniture was until that day. I had bought it all brand new when we moved into this house. The guys who delivered everything set it up just like I wanted it. After that, Jacob had always moved things for me.

Once we were done with the heavy stuff, I still had to figure out what to do with all my photos. It would've been impractical to throw away everything with his face on it. Most of the pictures we had were family photos with Jacob, me, and the kids. I decided to put everything into photo boxes until I could decide what to do with it. Jada had to have known how uncomfortable I was and how hard this was for me. We talked a lot. I finally began to let down the wall that Jada accused me of having up for so long.

I was very proud of myself by the end of the day because I only cried once. There was a portrait of our family in the upstairs hallway that had been taken less than six months prior. Around that time was when we began to make plans for our summer vacation. I still remember Jacob telling me how he was more in love with me than he had ever been. He said I had never looked more beautiful than I did on that day. I studied that picture for a while to see what it was I had missed. Was his smile crooked? Or was he just able to lie to me with a straight face by then? Did he know then that Salihah was on her way? I couldn't figure it out. I just decided to take it down and put it in the attic. Half way up the steps, I burst into tears. Jada helped me off the ladder and took the portrait up herself. There were more memories up there than I was probably ready to face, anyway.

We were both exhausted and decided to break for lunch at around one o'clock. The upstairs hallway, bathrooms, and my bedroom were all done. We were beginning to think we probably wouldn't get to the living room or anything else downstairs before the boys got home from school. Cooking was out of the question, so Jada ran to get us some fast food while I took a quick break on my couch. I was trying to figure out exactly what I wanted to do with the living room and the front den when the phone rang.

"Hello."

Even without looking at the caller ID, I was sure it was the school or the daycare. I figured it was only a matter of time before one of my boys began acting out because of all of the extra stress at home. I prepared myself for the questions I was sure I was about to be asked. 'Ms. Peterson, has your family undergone any kind of major change lately? Has your son been exposed to any sort of unusual stress?' I must've been lost in my thought, because I almost didn't even hear the person on the other end of the line introduce herself.

"Ms. Peterson?"

"Yes."

"This is Mrs. Hackerman at Prestige National Bank. How are you?"

"I'm fine, Mrs. Hackerman…what can I do for you?" I'm sure she sensed my confusion. I was a bit nervous. I hadn't heard from the bank since over a year ago when we were behind on the note. I knew that couldn't be the case this time, because Jacob had assured me he paid the house note at the beginning of the month. Now I was really nervous. What else had he been lying to me about?

"Well, I know it may seem a bit odd for me to be contacting you, but there was a rather sizable payment made toward your loan today. I have to follow the bank's policy whenever a payment this large is made. We need to be sure that you gave permission for the payment."

"I'm sorry…payment? You've lost me Mrs. Hackerman."

"Well, Ms. Peterson, apparently you have a friend who must carry you in the highest esteem. A man by the name of Mr. Owodunni made a payment covering the pay off amount of your home loan today. He was insistent that you not know until tomorrow, but as I just told you, it's bank policy to –"

"I'm sorry, Mrs. Hackerman. Did you just say he paid off the entire loan?"

"Well, yes, ma'am. However, if you were not aware of the payment or didn't authorize him to –"

"Mrs. Hackerman, I'm sorry to keep interrupting you, but let me just say that it's more than okay for Mr. Owodunni to have made that payment. Do you need me to come sign anything? Or is my word alone enough?"

"Well, since I have spoken to you, I can move forward processing the paperwork. You will just have to sign the title once the payment clears. Since the payment is so large, it will probably take anywhere from 10-15 business days. Once I have the title ready for you, I'll contact you again."

"Thank you so much for calling Mrs. Hackerman. If there is anything else I can help with, please don't hesitate to call."

With that, my day went from good to better. I was still in shock by the time Jada got back with the food.

"Girl, have you even moved from that spot since I left."

"Nah, I'm too busy admiring my beautiful home which, according to the bank, has just been paid off."

"Huh? Now I know you were tired when I left, but dang! Girl, are you startin' to have hallucinations? What do you mean paid off? I didn't think you had that kind of money saved up. Hell, if so I would've gotten a loan from you a long time ago."

"No, Jada. Not me. Someone from the bank just called and said Jacob made a payment today that covered the payoff amount of the house! I can't believe it myself, but I just had to say it out loud to see how it felt."

"Well, well, well. Mr. Jacob has come finally come through! Are you sure it was him? Did she describe him?"

"Girl, how many Owodunni's could there be in this city? Hell, I don't care if it was Mr. Ed! If he's givin' away free money, I'm takin' it!"

"Yeah, Mo', but what if it's not free? What if Jacob is up to somethin'? You better call him. Or at least call the bank and tell them to hold the payment until you can figure out what's up."

"Look, Jada, I appreciate your opinion, and I hear what you're saying. As far as I'm concerned, Jacob has gotten all he's gonna get from me. I don't care what he wants. He pretty much owed it to me to pay off this house. After all I've done for him over the last five years, how did he show his gratitude? He abandoned me and his only son just so he could choose the child with a purer bloodline! I have had to explain all this madness to our child...no...to BOTH of our children while he is off gallivanting with his new sex toy! He doesn't have the right to ask me for another thing! I deserve this! Screw a ring. She can have *his* sorry ass. I get to live my life with one less...no...two less worries now. Fact of the matter is, I need to write lil' Ms. Salihah a thank you letter. As far as me ever calling him, I wouldn't even give him the satisfaction. I have made my last attempt to contact him about anything. The only thing he and I have to talk about is Jackson. *He* can call *me* for that!"

Jada didn't protest. She knew I meant every word I said. Fact of the matter was that I wasn't saying anything that she or my family weren't probably thinking already. I knew how hard it was for everyone to accept my relationship with Jacob. The one thing that had held us together was that I knew he loved me. That was what was so hard. To have to find out that the man I had devoted so much to could do something like this to me was just devastating. I felt like the last five years of my life had all been a lie. I had convinced myself that the schemes Jacob pulled in his business life didn't have anything to do with me. I saw how genuine he was when dealing with his family. I figured some of that got passed along to me. I suppose I was always an outsider. He was just really good at making me feel like I wasn't.

"Mo, do you know what you're gonna do with the rooms down here?" I guess she just decided to change the subject since I had said all there was to say.

"Well, I know I need to redo the den first, 'cause that's where I'll be working. Other than that, I really don't have any ideas. Plus, I'm pooped! Let's just eat and talk about it later."

"I'm all for that, girl!"

We ate and talked some more then Jada went with me to pick up the boys. We spent the rest of the afternoon shopping for stuff for my den. I told Jada she had helped enough for one day and that I would redo the den on my own once I got home. We found some really great bargains while we were out. It felt totally different shopping for a house that was already paid for. I must admit that part of me wanted to call Jacob and thank him. I didn't have any problems fighting off that urge. All I had to do was think about what had just transpired one day earlier. Plus, I was still in shock. I refused to believe what I had heard until I saw some sort of proof. I mean, for all I knew, Jacob had just paid someone to call me and say the house was paid off. Who was to say what kinds of games he wouldn't play with my emotions at this point? There was no question that he had enough money for this to actually be true, though. I had received word through the grapevine that Jacobs marriage to lil' Miss Perfect had gotten him more than just a baby. Apparently, her father had given them a $300,000 wedding gift. That plus the birth of their first child was enough to ensure Jacob a long life of prosperity with the princess of his mother's dreams. I suppose every man has his price. What I didn't understand is why Jacob would use it to pay off my house. The payoff amount on my home loan was still well over $200,000. Jacob would have had to spend almost the entire dowry. That wasn't my problem. I had a decorating bug I had to appease.

I cooked dinner and helped Mathieu with his homework. Once the boys were in bed, I got a burst of energy. I decided to finish the den. While working, I got a call from Jada.

"Hey, girl. I was just callin' to check on you. Have you made any progress on the den yet?"

"Well, I'm still burnin' this midnight oil, but I should be done in another hour or so. I really like how the paintings look in this room. The pillows match my chairs perfectly, too."

Jada and I had bought a lot of black art to put in the room. I decided to give the room a new feel with some different throw pillows and a new cover for the small love seat.

"I'm so glad to see that everything is working out like you wanted. I'll have to come by tomorrow and see it. I think I'll stop by on my way from the gym. We can have lunch."

"Sounds great!"

We never knew how to end a conversation. We talked for the next two hours until I finished the room.

Chapter Thirteen
The Eighth Day

I woke up Wednesday morning with a new energy. I didn't know if it was the news I had gotten about the house, the redecorating, or the conversation I had with Jada. Whatever it was, I felt alive for the first time in over a week.

I got up, looked around my house, and felt like a kid on Christmas morning. The whole house had a new atmosphere. I finally felt like I was going to make it on my own. The thought of being by myself was no longer frightening. It was exciting! I made breakfast for the boys as they began to slowly rise from their deep slumbers. Mathieu always took the longest to get ready. All Jackson had to do was smell food, and that was enough motivation for him to get dressed in a hurry. As they came downstairs to eat, I noticed that they both seemed to be trying to take in all the newness of the house. It's amazing the difference a couple of new pictures and throws can make. Their bedrooms hadn't been changed. There was no need. Plus, I wanted them both to have a comfortable place to rest amidst all the madness that was going on around them. Everyone needs a sanctuary. Children are no different.

"Mama?"

"Yes, Jackson." Okay, I thought. Here we go. I knew the kids would both have non-stop questions about Jacob. How was I going to handle this? What was I supposed to say?

"Is daddy going to die?"

"Huh?" I almost choked on my pancakes. "Jackson, baby, why would you ask that?"

"Well, when Paw-paw died, Grandma bought new pillows for her couch. She put up new curtains, too. So is daddy gonna die? Like Paw-paw did?"

I was shocked at his innocent view of the situation. When my father died, my mother put up some new curtains and throws that my dad said he hated when he was alive. She had put them up years earlier and had to take them down because she and he disagreed so badly about the issue. I suppose once he died, that was her way of having the last word. She came home once and found one of the throw pillows in the middle of the floor. No one knew how it got there. My mom joked that it had been my dad's ornery way of still arguing with her from the grave. I never thought about relating my situation to any of that. Kids have the most unique ways of seeing things. I didn't know whether I wanted to cry or laugh, but I knew I had to maintain my composure or he would sense something was wrong. The last thing I wanted to do was confuse him anymore.

"Well, baby, it is true that your grandmother did those things. I know you've noticed that mommy put up some new stuff in our house. That's all it is, though, Jackson. It's just new stuff. Now remember that mommy told you daddy went live with his new family now. He is over at your Grandma Mani's house. As far as I know he will not be dying anytime soon. Mommy just wanted to make some changes at our house."

"Okay. But when we change my room, can I have all Batman stuff?"

Whew. I had barely escaped that one. I didn't know if he really understood or if he just wanted me to think he did. Jackson had wisdom well beyond his years, but he would often change the subject when he didn't understand something and come back to it after he had taken the time to ponder over it. I was hoping he was doing more understanding and less pondering, but I wasn't going to push the subject.

"So, Mathieu, do you have any requests for your room?"

"No ma'am. I want everything to stay the same."

"Great! So Batman for Jackson and no changes for

Mathieu. I can live with that."

Mathieu was a completely different ball of wax. He was very introverted. I think he got that from me. He very seldom talked about how he felt, but I could see this was taking a toll on him. The hardest thing about his situation was that he knew Jacob was not his real father. Their relationship had been wonderful since Jacob was the only father he'd ever known other than my dad. Their bond was tested pretty strongly once Jacob's mother moved in with us. Kumani had never missed an opportunity to point out the fact that Mathieu was not Jacob's biological son. Jacob and I had lots of long talks with him during that time. He always felt like Jacob was his father no matter what Kumani said in front of him. I could only imagine what kinds of thoughts must have been going through his head now.

"So, Mathieu, isn't your math test today?"

"Yes, ma'am."

"Are you ready? Do you want to do some more practice problems this morning before you go?"

"No ma'am. I'm fine. We did this same stuff last week, but some of the kids didn't do so well, so Mrs. Hutchins says we all have to take the test again."

"Well, I'm sure you'll do just fine. Oh! I really need you to be ready when I come pick you up today. We have a busy afternoon. Your brother has soccer practice, and we have to pick up your cousin from band practice at her school. Your Aunt Lena and Uncle Brock are going out tonight, so Brook and Bailey are joining us for dinner."

"Yeah! I get to go to the big kids' school!" Jackson was always excited to go with me to pick up anyone from school. "Mommy, can we have pizza for dinner tonight?"

"I'll think about it Jackson. Let's just see what happens after we pick up your cousins. The girls may not want pizza."

"They never want pizza. I hate girls." Mathieu grumbled.

I could tell he was trying to perk up. No matter how much he grumbled and complained, I knew he loved it when the girls came over. I just wished I could pass on my newfound excitement to him. That's another hard thing about parenting. Not being able to shield your children from all the hurts of life. The most you can usually do is guide them through it and be there to pick up any pieces that may fall along the way. In a way, I was glad he had his cousins. They knew what it was like with Brock being out of town all the time. While this was a very different situation, at least he had someone to relate to.

"So, boys, is everybody done with breakfast?"

"Yes, ma'am." They sang in unison.

"Okay, get your book bags, and let's go." I quickly cleared the dishes as they raced to see who would be first to the car.

Mathieu and I had some one on one time after I dropped Jackson off at the daycare. He asked a couple of questions about Jacob. He told me that he was okay with us not being together. I guess it's the mother in me that wanted to dig deeper, but I left it at that. I knew we would have plenty of time to talk about everything. I wasn't going to try to conquer it all in one morning.

I got back to the house just before eight thirty. I turned on the morning news to see what had been going on in the world since I'd been in hiding. After that, I dusted off one of my old Pilates DVD's and got to work. I figured if I was going be single that I might as well be sexy while doing so. After about fifteen minutes or so, I was satisfied that I was sexy enough for one day. Once you step away from a work out like that, it's hard to get back into it. After a quick shower, I put on what I call my gypsy skirt. It was a long skirt with tiny little metal balls hand-sewn at the hem. They hung down from underneath the skirt and jingled when I walked. I loved the way I felt when I wore that skirt. It was like a total transformation. That was what I felt like I needed. I put on my head wrap and matching accessories. As I looked in the mirror, I had to laugh. I already knew what Jada would say when she saw me. She hated this outfit and refused to go anywhere with me when I wore it. While I thought I looked exotic and beautiful, she swore the head wrap made me look like Aunt Jemima. I would deal with Jada later. I decided to turn on some music and do the breakfast dishes while I made up my mind what to do with myself until lunchtime.

I was in the middle of Patti Labelle's declaration of *her* new attitude when I heard someone beating on my front door. I hadn't heard the vehicle pull up because I had the headset of my iPod turned almost all the way up. The poor person on the other side must've rang the doorbell a million times before deciding to just beat down the door in the hopes that whoever was inside was not deaf or dead. I danced over to the door and stopped dead in my tracks once I opened it.

"Can I come in?"

"Go ahead. Apparently it's your house now."

"Oh, so you know about that."

"Yeah, I do, Jacob. I know about most of the secrets you've tried to keep from me over the last few months. Are you here to give me the dish on the rest?"

"Shamonica, the reason I came here is to let you know that you can pick up the deed to the house next week. The loan officer at the bank pushed the paperwork through faster than what they thought they would. The payment has cleared and all you will have to do is sign the final set of papers declaring your ownership of the house."

"Well, I'm sure someone at the bank would've been happy to call and let me know that once they opened. Since you insisted on coming to tell me anyway, I'm going to assume you have something else to say."

He had moved from outside the doorway to standing next to me in the foyer. I just stood there, still in the doorway, with my hand on the doorknob. I did not intend for him to get one step further into my domain. I had given up enough to this man. I felt space was a very small favor to ask at that point.

"I don't even know why you came here. The boys are gone, and I certainly don't want to see you!"

"Shamonica, why does it always have to be a battle with you? I'm trying to make this more bearable, and it's like you just want to make it hard."

My eyes widened in amazement at his audacity. He had managed to keep a straight face, so I was pretty sure he actually believed the garbage that had just fallen from his lips.

"*I'm* making this hard! There wouldn't even be a 'this' if you had been honest with me years ago and just let me know you didn't want me! I didn't ask to have to deal with this shit! You did this! All of it! You were the one who said you loved me! You said that God had created me specifically for you and *only* you! You convinced me that we belonged together, and now you want to stand in *my* house and tell me that *I'm* making something hard? You made it look pretty damn easy to me, Jacob. Matter of fact, it seemed down right effortless how you fucked another woman behind my back for months and then left me for her! How hard was it really, Jacob? Tell me!"

His head dropped and seemed to sink more with every syllable out of my mouth. The angry little black woman began to rise up, but this time she would have to take a back seat. I had a lot to get off of my chest, and I didn't intend to let her steal my thunder.

"Jacob, all I did…all I ever did, was love you. I gave you a family. I helped build you a business. Hell, I would've given you anything in the world that I even *thought* you needed! I thought you would do that for me, too. My family and my friends said you weren't right for me and I loved you anyway. What I felt for you was real. I saw something in you that nobody else seemed to see. I know you saw things in me, too. I thought we were growing…together. I tried to build on our bond and cultivate it into something strong that the both of us could depend on. You told me you wanted the same thing. You *told* me that what we had meant something to you, and then you just spit on the relationship like it was nothing…like *I* was nothing! I have gone to the ends of the earth and back for you! All I asked was for you to love and respect me in return. You failed me twice."

"Shamonica...I –"

"No, Jacob! No!"

I felt the white hot burning of my eyes about to give way to yet more tears. This time there would be no mourning. What I needed was a cleansing. I was going to have to get it all out if I ever planned to move forward with my life.

"You will not take control of this situation! You will stand there, and you will listen to me! When I'm done, Jacob, you will leave!"

"Let's just go into the den where we can talk. I don't want our conversation blasted over the entire neighborhood."

He looked almost like a child who knew he was about to face punishment. I had been with him for five years and never seen this man look like that. Somehow, that didn't matter to me.

"Oh, did you not want to blast it all over the neighborhood when you and your brother moved all your stuff out of the house while I was at work? Did you not want the neighborhood to know about your little wifey when you brought her ass to my house? This whole damn thing has all been played out for the neighborhood anyway, so let's just give 'em the grand fuckin' finale, Jacob!"

"Shamonica, it doesn't have to be like this."

He looked at me pleading with his eyes for me to just hear what he was saying. The same way I must've looked at him so many times before when I needed him to understand my point of view. It's a very different feeling. Knowing you have the power to control a person's insides from where you're standing. That kind of power can be deadly in the wrong hands. I knew. I had given Jacob that power for five years. It was my turn to prove I wasn't anything like him.

I slowly shut the door and we proceeded to the den. On the way there, we passed the library where Jacob used to spend most of his time when he lived in the house. I looked at the rows of empty or semi-empty shelves where his books used to be. He had also taken his desk, which had been a birthday gift from me a few years back. I hadn't paid much attention to the items missing from that room over the eight days that Jacob had been gone. Him being in the house that day and those things not being there just reinforced the fact that he was a visitor. This was not a happy homecoming. There would never be one. This house would have to readjust like every one of its inhabitants.

"You took down our pictures."

Jacob was noticing the den as if it was brand new. Taking in every detail as if he had never seen it before. Trying, I'm sure, to grasp something familiar to link himself to so he wouldn't be so uncomfortable. He would have no such luck. I had removed all reminders of him from this space and had no regrets about doing so.

"Yeah, I did. You can have 'em if you like. Oh, no... silly me! You probably have your wedding pictures up at your place already."

"Look, 'Mo, can't we just talk without all the animosity?"

"Animosity?" I chuckled, "I don't know what you mean. I don't have any animosity toward you. No, Jacob! See, that would require me to give a damn about you. I don't anymore."

My tone was as cold as dry ice. I had no intention of him seeing any sign of weakness. It had been bad enough almost getting emotional at the door, but this was my time. I wanted to let him know he couldn't break me.

"I'm sorry to hear that."

"Oh, really?"

"Yes. I am."

"And why is that Jacob?"

"Because I still love you very much."

He never moved. Never blinked. He just stood there looking at me. He wanted a reaction. He needed me to give him a sign that I still had feelings for him. Much the same way I needed him to prove his commitment to me by marrying me. We were both on an even keel as far as chances of either of those things happening. I had no intentions on giving him any ease to the conscience that must have been weighing on him as heavily as my grief had been weighing on me.

"What do you want me to say, Jacob? You want me to tell you I love you, too? You want us to just pretend like none of this ever happened and move forward? What the hell is wrong with you? First you don't want me, now you're standing here telling me you love me? You're **married** for God's sake! Does your **wife** even know you came here?"

"I never said I didn't want you, Shamonica. You're all I want. You are all I have ever wanted. I just wish I could —"

He actually stopped mid-sentence like he didn't know what to say. This was unusual. I looked into the eyes of the man who had been my strong tower for so long and I saw him crumbling.

"Mo', everything you said was true. You did give me all those things. I just wish you knew that I sacrificed for you as well. I would never tell you so, because I love you too much. It hasn't always been easy to be with you, but I stayed because I was just as much in love with you as you were with me. When this thing started out, I was making an attempt to provide for my family – you, Mathieu, and Jackson. Things happened that weren't supposed to, and

I had some very tough decisions that I had to make. I can take responsibility for my mistakes, but the one thing I will always regret is hurting you. Shamonica, you are the only woman I have ever loved, and there is nothing I wouldn't do for you. My decision to get married had nothing to do with my feelings for you. I just got lost. I had no other choice. Maybe if I were some kind of superman, this would be easy. The problem is that I'm not Superman. I am only a man - a very foolish one. I can't make you believe me. If I were you, I wouldn't want to see me either. I just had to tell you that I still love you. I haven't thought about anything but you ever since I left this home…our home."

"Look, Jacob, if that was your attempt at an apology, save it! I don't know what kind of game you're trying to play, but this is my *life*. I don't need to hear this right now. I'm in the middle of a celebration of self, and I don't need to hear your violins playing at my party. I have just successfully completed a project that I poured my soul into for the last five months. Need I remind you, Jacob, that for four of those months, while I thought I had your complete support, you were gallivanting around with another woman? I still made it. I did it all on my own. I didn't need your help, your love, or your support as badly as I thought I did after all. I have taken your best shot, Jacob, and I'm still standing. You can't hurt me anymore. It's over. Stop trying to find a place in my life. There is nothing here for you. Just get out of my house! You can see your son whenever you want, but you and I have nothing else to discuss. That's the way this is going to be! *You* will just have to **deal** with it!" I was walking swiftly toward the front door to let him out when I felt him grab my arm.

"Mo, wait!"

I looked into the eyes of the man I had just wounded. He was slowly dying inside. I could tell. There was no life in his eyes like there used to be. Even his overall appearance was disheveled. This wasn't the Jacob I was used to. I wondered how long it had been since he'd slept. He hadn't even shaved. It had only been four days since I last laid eyes on him, but I could've sworn he had gained a pound or two. He looked as if years of hardship had overtaken him all at once.

"Shamonica, I need you."

"Let me go, Jacob."

I was beginning to feel the pain that a person feels when someone they love is hurting. It's a connection to a person that defies description. It's much the same as a mother who knows when something is wrong with her child or a twin who just feels that the other twin is in trouble. My eyes began to cry first his tears, then my own. My heart was heavy with his longing. I fully understood the need he was expressing. It was the same need I had lain in bed with every night since the night he left me. That kind of need doesn't just go away. Even with the presence of another person, you still feel the void. It's not sexual, but spiritual. I believe that's why God intended marriage to be forever. You can't just break that kind of bond and not expect to face dire consequences. This was the bond I had wanted to protect so badly. In the end, I suppose, Jacob had no respect for our connection or for me. I don't even know if he had noticed it until he didn't have me anymore. As far as I was concerned, he was just reaping all that he had sown. I wished I could just stop loving him long enough to enjoy seeing it. There was no pleasure for me in this. All I felt was pain…both his and mine.

"Mo', I miss my friend. I miss the woman who used to believe in me. I miss our talks and even the nights that we'd just lay together on the couch and never said a word. I miss the smell of your hair and the feeling of having your head lying on my chest. Mo', I miss *us*."

My breathing was heavy as I listened to him rattle off small details of our life. They played back in my mind like a movie. I knew those things were just fairy tales. The harsh reality was that he would have to get used to the smell of someone else's hair on his pillow. I didn't have any control over that. When he could have done something to change it, he chose not to. I had lost that battle without even getting the opportunity to strike a blow.

He slowly let his hand slide down my arm and grabbed my hand. I turned my head, but couldn't pull my hand away. I looked up toward the ceiling to ask God to help me. I still craved this man. I wanted to hold him and tell him everything was okay. That would have been a lie. Everything was anything but okay. I tried to think of something else while he was talking. I just wanted to drown out his words long enough to get back to my happy place. The place I had been all morning before he interrupted me.

"I know I messed up! There is nothing I can do about that. I want to make it right, somehow. I know I can't, but I just want to. You have to know that I never meant to hurt you. You don't have to believe me. Just tell me you can at least understand that much. Please, just give me that. Look at me, Mo'. Can't you even look at me?"

"You don't miss me, Jacob. You just think you do. Guilt can play crazy tricks on your mind." Even with tears streaming down my face, I was seeing very clearly at that moment. I tried to get a few steps closer to the front door. Jacob had to go. There would be no negotiating. It was pointless.

Jacob pulled me back and kissed me with a passion more intense than I recall ever feeling from him. It was like he had years of unspoken words that he was now trying to express in a totally different way. He pushed me against the wall where I stood and began to touch my body like he used to when we were still in love. My body felt like all was right again. If my mind hadn't known better, I might have been able to believe it as well. I felt his soft lips make their way down my neck and toward my cleavage. I now stood with my back against the wall looking into the library. If not for the tears blinding my eyes, I probably would have been able to see out the window. I was sure that was where my moment of clarity had gone – right out the window. I longed for that clarity again. Just some hint of something that made sense so that I could relieve the pounding in my head.

"Jacob, we can't do this. It's not right." I shook my head, but my hands interlocked with his and I kissed him back with the same intensity he had shown me. My mind and my mouth had said no, but it was clear that they were not in control. My heart and body took over and began to do what felt natural.

"Shamonica I need you." He was now breathless. Beads of sweat were forming on his brow.

"But you **chose** her!"

My crying was even more out of control. My body responded to kisses I had been longing for since the last time I had felt them. *Damn him for giving me a chance to feel this again. Why won't he just leave me alone?*

"I will never love anyone but you." He whispered in my ear as he wiped the never-ending stream of tears from my face. He planted kisses on my cheeks as if to try and stop their flow.

"I hate you."

I had been broken down to a silent whisper. Jacob probably knew my body better than I did. He used that knowledge to its fullest extent. I was so excited I couldn't even think straight. It was like I had lost total control of my own body. I pulled him in closer to me until our bodies had no space in between them. The gentle tinkering of the gypsy skirt's chimes echoed in my ears as a hot passionate whirlwind began to blow. I stood outside myself and watched him kiss the vessel I had once inhabited. She lifted her floor length skirt and allowed Jacob to once again enter her soul. I had cried oceans, and I heard the frantic beating of the tides of those oceans as Jacob brought my empty vessel to climax. He had once again proven that this was his territory. Now it was time for me to reclaim mine.

I attempted to return to my happy place. I tried to think about anything other than the pleasure of the throbbing I now felt between my thighs. I was breathless and exhausted from the intensity of the act itself. My mind raced in circles trying to figure out what had just happened. Somewhere in the whirlwind resurfaced the thought of who he was. He was the man who had hurt me. He was the person who had taken all of me and crushed it. Most important of all, he was the man who had gotten married just two days prior. I slid slowly down the wall and allowed the floor to catch me. I barely spoke above a whisper, but my message was very clear.

"Get out."

Chapter Fourteen
Taking It All Back

I heard the door close softly as Jacob left my home. He must have sat in his truck for a minute before deciding to drive off, because it seemed like forever before I heard the Chevy's roaring engine. On my way upstairs to take my shower, I slowly took in every room in my house. I wanted to make note of every detail. I asked myself what I liked and what I didn't like. I began to make plans for the library to become the boys' study. I would not allow myself to think about the event that had just transpired. When I got out of the shower, I made myself a cup of hot tea and turned on my CD player. I had just bought a few CD's that I hadn't had time to listen to. As I prepared to allow the lyrics of Lupe Fiasco to penetrate my mind, I noticed an envelope underneath the player. It was a card in a Hallmark envelope. Only God knows when Jacob had hidden it there. He was always doing things like that.

He would hide gifts and cards in common places hoping that they would be overlooked. When a special date came around, he would pop up with gifts from all over the house. This card was apparently for our anniversary. It had my name on the front. I was fighting the urge to open it. I spoke my thoughts out loud just to reinforce their importance. I sounded like somebody talking to the screen during a scary movie.

"Mo, get a grip! Don't open the card, girl."

I stuffed it into the oversized pocket of my robe and tuned in to my CD. The next artists on the list were Lyfe Jennings and Chingy. I planned to get my party on all by myself. This was truly my celebration of ME. I pulled out a stack of old mail that I had been meaning to go through. After I paid a few bills online, I started getting ready for lunch with Jada. This day was my time and mine alone. Still there was a funny feeling in the pit of my stomach that I couldn't shake. I made myself ignore it because I was sure it was just the residue of my feelings for Jacob trying to creep their way back in. I resolved that nothing was going to ruin my day, and continued my festivities. I was dressed over an hour too early, but I didn't care. I just decided to sit on my couch looking fabulous until she called. I pulled out a bottle of wine that had been chilling in preparation for me to celebrate my promotion. I poured myself a glass as Lyfe Jennings began to tell the story of his own relationships.

Just when the wine got good and the music got better, Jada pulled up in the driveway. I know she was shocked when she saw that I was already dressed.

"Girl, what kinda party you got goin' on in here?"

"Nah, not a party, girl. This is just a liberation."

"Is that the new Lyfe CD I hear? Girl, I've been meaning to check that out!"

"Yup. I haven't had time to listen to it 'cause I've been too busy with work. I decided to take a long deserved break today."

"A break, huh?"

Jada cut her eyes at me as she began to scan the living room. With the exception of a couple of small candles burning on my coffee table, the room was completely dark. My incense was burning in the other room, but the robust aroma seemed to fill the entire house.

"That's what I said. What? Are you goin' deaf now?" I gave her a hard look back and rolled my eyes.

"Nah, I ain't deaf. I ain't blind either. As a matter of fact, *all* my senses are working just fine. And right now they are all telling me that you are tryin' to hide something."

"Hide? What would I have to hide?" I crossed my arms. "Girl, I'm a grown ass woman. Ain't no shame. If I had somethin' to say I'd say it."

I couldn't help blushing. Jada knew me all too well. Hell, for all I knew, the smell of sex was still in the air.

"Well, Ms. Growny, I'll be sittin' right here when you get ready to spill it. I'm not movin' until you do, so I suggest you make it snappy. I'm hungry as hell." She plopped down on the couch.

"Jada quit playin'! Come on now! I'm ready to go."

"The only person playin' in this room is you. Now who is he? The only time I've ever seen you this relaxed was the first time you and Jacob...GIRL NO YOU DIDN'T!!! He was here wasn't he? Ooh! Girl, you are goin' to hell with gasoline drawers on! I don't believe it!"

"Don't believe what?" I couldn't hide it anymore. The jig was up. I burst out laughing. "It's not what you think, girl. It wasn't even like that."

"Wasn't like what? All I said was he came over here. And anyway, you know it was *just* like that! He brought his married ass over here and tightened you up. Now you runnin' around drinkin' wine and listenin' to music wit' incense burnin' an' shit! Next week I'll come over here and you'll be playin' yo' Lenny and Luther in the dark while you sip on hard liquor." We both laughed.

"No Jada. Don't say that. This is not going to be a repeat thing. Trust me! Once was more than enough. I just had a moment of weakness. Anyway, the music and all that has nothing to do with Jacob. I really just wanted to unwind. I needed a break. Half the stuff over there is rap. You just happened to come in while I was listenin' to this. In any event, Girl, I don't think he'll want to come back. I came down on him pretty hard. He left with his tail between his legs."

"Nah, baby. He is still a man. He left here with a soft, wet dick between his legs. That alone is enough to make him want to come back. Mark my words Mo', if you don't cut this out now, there's going to be hell to pay in the long run. Now you can ignore me if you want to, but you'll remember I said this one-day. Hopefully sooner than later."

"Okay. I'm listenin', but just hear me out. I'm really trying hard to work my way through this. What happened today was a big mistake. I knew that before we did it. I can deal with the consequences of what happened, but what I'm *not* about to do is become the other woman. When Jacob had me full time, he didn't love me enough to make me his wife. Now I'll be damned if he makes me play second fiddle to his little princess. He made his choice and I intend to make him stick to it."

"Well, I'm glad to hear you say that. But, sis, please look out for yourself. I told you when he paid the house off that you didn't know what he had in mind. Just be aware that he knows you inside and out. Be careful when you deal with him. You never know what kind of shit he might try to pull later on if he feels insulted by you rejecting him."

"Okay, okay! Enough of this serious talk. Can we please go eat? A sista is starvin'!"

Jada walked toward the front door as I blew out the candles and turned off my CD player. I had truly taken in all of what she said. I just didn't feel like consuming another day of my life with thoughts of Jacob.

I did a double take to be sure all the candles were out, and just as I did, the phone rang.

"Hello."

"Yes, Ms. Peterson?"

"Yes, Janice, is everything okay?" This was the call from the daycare I had been waiting on. I braced myself for what I was about to hear. I thought I did, anyway.

"Ms. Peterson, I am so sorry to have to call you with bad news, but it's Jackson. He's being taken to the hospital. Now, I don't want you to panic –"

"Janice, if you don't want me to panic, then don't start your conversation telling me my son is in a hospital! What happened? Was there an accident? Is he hurt? What's going on?" *Oh, my God, this was the feeling I couldn't shake.*

"No, ma'am. It's nothing like that. He complained of a stomach ache shortly after you dropped him off. He did tell me that he had pancakes at home this morning, so I just figured he'd eaten too much syrup or something like that. I sent him in to my nurse to rest for a while, but the pain got worse. Once she assessed that there was nothing we could do for him here, I called for an ambulance. They are still here now. I called you once I got off the phone with the 911 operator. My nurse is going to ride to the hospital with him, but I wanted to call you as soon as possible so that you could meet them there. Ms. Peterson, let me assure you that we are doing everything we can to..."

I couldn't comprehend anything else. My baby was in an ambulance on his way to a hospital...without me. I couldn't imagine how afraid he must've been. I knew Janice's nurse very well. She and I had actually gone to high school together. In fact, she had been the one to refer me to Janice's daycare. I knew she was qualified to do her job, but somehow that didn't ease my fear. I needed to go be with my child.

"Janice, thank you for calling me. Just tell Terri I'll meet her at the hospital. I have to go."

"I understand. I'll actually be meeting you there as well. I just have to call in a couple of my staff to come in before I can leave. Again, Ms. Peterson, I'm very sorry, but I'm sure everything is going to be just fine. There is just one more thing–"

"Mo, will you come on? I told you I'm hungry." I

had forgotten that Jada was outside waiting for me. I was so glad that she was, because there was no way I could drive.

"I'm sorry, Janice, I know you'll understand, but I need to leave now. Whatever it is, I'm sure it can wait."

"Of course, Ms. Peterson, I'll see you at the hospital."

∾

We made it to the hospital just in time to see the ambulance pull up. They wouldn't let me go back to the exam rooms, but Terri was able to come out and talk to me once Jackson was in a bed. I had to stay in the waiting area and fill out forms. Actually, Jada ended up filling them out. I was pacing and waiting for someone to tell me what was going on with my baby. Terri showed up and immediately began dishing details as if on cue.

"Shamonica, calm down. I know this is a lot to take in, but Jackson needs you to stay calm. From what I can see, he is exhibiting all the classic signs of appendicitis. Now it's rare in kids his age, but not unheard of. If the doctors here agree with me, the only cure is going to be for them to perform an appendectomy."

"Terri, they can't cut on my baby! He's just a baby! Oh, my God –"

"Shamonica, that's only my assessment of the situation.

That's why I told Janice to call the ambulance instead of us bringing him here or waiting for you to pick him up. We needed to get him here as soon as possible to be able to confirm it before something bad happened. I know it's a lot to take in, but just wait until you hear what his doctor has to say. I only want you to be ready in case they confirm what I'm thinking. I promise you I will stay here the whole time. I'm not going anywhere, and if you have any questions or you don't understand what they're saying to you, I'm here to help. I promise. Nothing bad is going to happen to Jackson – not while I'm here."

"You're standing here telling me they might have to operate on my baby, Terri. That's bad!"

"Operate? On **my** son? What are you talking about? What's going on?"

I turned to see Jacob right behind me as if we had invited him to take part in our conversation. Terri saw the bewilderment on my face and correctly guessed that Janice hadn't gotten to tell me that "one more thing" she wanted to express over the phone.

"Jacob's cell number was the primary emergency number in Jackson's file, Shamonica. We didn't even know you guys weren't together until today. I thought Janice was telling you when I was leaving that he was going to be here too."

"I don't need an explanation for why I'm here, Terri.

He's **my** son. I don't need you to apologize for my presence as if I don't belong here." Jacob huffed.

"Look, Jacob," I was not in the mood for theatrics "we're all here for the same reason. Jackson needs us. Please don't come in here acting like that. Terri is only trying to do her job." I was proud of how I had diffused the situation until I saw Salihah and Kumani walk in and take seats right behind Jada. Before I could react, I turned to see Jackson's doctor approaching.

"Mr. and Mrs. Peterson —"

"Ms. Peterson" I shook his hand before Jacob had time to comment.

"Yes, well, you two are Jackson's parents, correct?"

"Yes" we spoke in unison.

"Well, you should probably thank your nurse here for bringing Jackson in so quickly. He does indeed have acute appendicitis, and we'll need to get him into an OR as soon as possible. Now he's a very bright young boy. Wise beyond his years, and he's very strong. I don't foresee any problems or complications. Does he have any chronic health conditions I should be aware of?"

"No" I stated as Jacob looked at me for an answer.

"Good, then. I'll let you two go in to see him and we can get him prepped for surgery. I'll explain the procedure now, or you can wait until we are in the room with Jackson in case he has questions. Something tells me he will."

"You can explain in front of Jackson," I said. "He's always been fascinated with medicine. I'm sure he'll want to know exactly what is going to happen."

"Good, then. If you two will follow me this way…" He motioned toward the exam rooms and Jacob and I followed.

All I wanted at that moment was to see my baby. I didn't care what else the doctor said. I suppose I should've been relieved once he walked us through the surgery step-by-step, but instead it just made me more apprehensive. Eventually, I resolved that this was what had to be done, and decided there was no use appearing worried in front of my son. Jackson asked enough questions for us all. He was actually excited. Funny thing, but children really do have the most unique way of looking at the world. In my opinion, boys are even more unique thinkers than girls when it comes to this. Jackson's excitement was over the scars he would have on his belly afterwards. He said he couldn't wait to show his class at show-and-tell once he got back to Ms. Janice's. Seeing him crack a smile, even a weak one, was what I needed to get me through what seemed to be the longest wait of my life.

Once we returned to the waiting room, that smile was what I had to envision to keep me silent under the sarcastic stares of Jacob's mother and even the silent smirks of his new wife. My family, Terri, and Janice all sat on one side of the room. Jacob's family sat on the other. Jada had gone to pick up Mathieu, Brook, and Bailey when it was time. She called my mother to let her know what was going on. My mother insisted that Jada bring her to the hospital to be with me. Of course, once Brock and Lena got word, they cancelled their plans to come be with us. It was decided that Jada would take the kids back to my house to finish homework and watch movies while we all waited. I was glad Jada wasn't there in a way. In other ways, I wanted her blood-boiling nature beside me. Only she knew my secret of what had gone on just a few hours prior. I imagined she and I shooting our own knowing looks in the direction of Kumani. It was a fleeting thought. All that was on the forefront of my mind was my baby. Not even my disdain over Jacob and his family could fully distract me from that. I got up to go to the bathroom just because I needed to walk. I couldn't stand all that waiting. I was getting stir crazy.

Once in the bathroom, I noticed how tired my eyes were beginning to look. I cupped cold water in my hands and splashed it on my face.

"Get it together, girl." I spoke at my own reflection as I dried my face with the cheap, scratchy paper towels provided beside the sink. My conversation was interrupted by another visitor entering. It was Salihah.

She stood shoulder to shoulder with me in the mirror

and began to primp her hair. I could've sworn I heard her "hmph" as she turned to go into the bathroom stall.

Don't do it Mo'. We gotta hold it together. She's not worth it. Just be cool and walk away.

I was taking another deep breath when Salihah let out a shrill scream that knocked me backwards a few steps. She was in the stall, so I couldn't see what she was yelling about, but I knew whatever it was, it was not good. There I was standing at the bathroom door with my hand on the handle to leave, and she was now wailing in a way that I've never heard any woman cry.

"Go get my husband! I need my husband! God help me, please!"

I wanted to move, but I was paralyzed. Kumani burst through the door and pushed me aside as if she had heard Salihah screaming from the waiting area. Right behind her was Jacob. The bathroom door began to close and stopped at my foot which was planted like lead in the same spot. Our eyes met, and I still couldn't move. He was responding to the cries of his wife. He was her husband. I was nobody. Just as my heart began to pound like it was going to jump out of my chest, Kumani spoke.

"WHAT DID YOU DO TO HER?" She spat at me, as if it were my fault all this was happening. I never moved from the spot I was in, but underneath the wall of the bathroom stall, I could see that there was blood on the floor in front of the toilet. I shuffled out of the bathroom quickly as if I had just seen a dead body. Jacob still stood there dumbfounded.

I walked past him toward the person I saw coming toward me. It was the doctor from the emergency room.

"Ms. Peterson, Jackson is out of surgery. He's in the recovery room, and he's doing fine. He's still a bit sleepy from the anesthesia, but he's been asking for his mommy."

"Can I go see my son?"

"Yes, you can. He can only have two visitors at a time, though. The recovery nurse is waiting to walk you back."

Kumani opened the bathroom door.

"Jacob! Your wife needs you! And bring a doctor!"

I never looked back. I grabbed my mother's hand and headed to my son's bedside. He needed me. I was his mother. That was all that mattered.

∽

Jackson was only in the hospital for two days. He had youth on his side, and the nurses said they had never had a better patient – pediatric or otherwise. Jackson kept them all in stitches with his questions and stories. I was just glad my baby was okay. Jacob never made it to the recovery room that night. He came to see Jackson once he was settled into a room upstairs. I never asked what had happened to Salihah or the baby, and I was glad he never offered. There was a look of defeat in his eyes when I saw him that was even deeper than the one he wore before our encounter. I didn't want to take up any more of my valuable time with him and his newfound family. I was just happy that my own son was happy and healthy again.

I called Mr. Kirkland and thanked him for the promotion, the raise, and the new office. I explained to him the circumstances surrounding Jackson's unfortunate emergency surgery. He assured me that Puerto Rico was not going anywhere and encouraged me to take all the time I needed to get my family back on track. Something about his tone told me that he understood more than what he was letting on. It just felt good to have somebody else in my corner.

The day I brought Jackson home, it was just like bringing him home from the hospital for the first time. I had made arrangements for things in his room to be just perfect when he got back. Brock, Lena, and the girls were more than happy to help out. Jackson made his way up to his room and squealed with delight at what he found.

"Bat-maaaaan!"

He jumped up and down so much I was scared he would tear his stitches.

J. Boss

"Be careful, Jackson. Don't you remember the doctors and nurses told you not to jump around until after we go see Dr. Morgan next week to take out your stitches?"

"Sorry, momma." He shot me a quick puppy-dog-eyed look before quickly returning to his excited cheers. Careful not to jump up and down, he slowly walked through his entire room admiring all the batman accessories.

I must say, Lena had outdone herself with this one. There were things in there that I hadn't even thought of. I left Jackson to play in his new room with another stern warning not to overdo it. I left the door open while I went to talk to Mathieu who we had picked up from Lena's on the way home. He was in his room drawing in his art book.

"Hey, you."

"Hey"

"So how's it going?"

"Okay, I guess." He never looked up from his drawings.

"You guess? Well tell me what's not okay. Maybe we can fix it."

"I doubt it." Now he was finally going to talk to me. I could feel it. I just didn't know what I was going to say back.

"Well, we'll never know unless you say something. I mean I can't fix everything, but at least if you tell me what's going on, then I'll know what we're working with. Then maybe we can try to fix it together."

"I just don't know why everybody is always tryin to change stuff - like when Grandpa died and just like when uncle Brock leaves all the time. Just when we get used to people being here, they go away. Why can't people just stay where they are?"

"Well, baby, you're right. I can't fix this one. And I know it hurts when people leave us. But what you have to remember is that it's never your fault. Uncle Brock has to leave because it's his job. Grandpa was old, and it was time for him to be with God –"

"What about Dad? He went to go live with his other family because he doesn't like me anymore. Just like Grandma Mani doesn't like me! Well I don't care! I don't like them, either! And I'm glad he's gone!" I couldn't hide anything at that moment. I was so shocked by his view of everything , not to mention his passion, that I just couldn't maintain my composure. All I could do was cry.

"Oh, baby! Baby! My precious! You listen to me." I scooped him up in my arms and held him like both our lives depended on it. "Jacob does not dislike you. I promise you that this has nothing to do with you. I can't make it all right, and I can't explain everything to you like I want to, but I promise you that it's not what you think. Jacob loves you very much, Mathieu and so do I. We would never do anything to hurt you on purpose. Grownups do stupid, stupid things sometimes, Baby. It's not your fault. But I promise you this: I will NEVER leave you." I grabbed his face and looked him right in the eyes to make my point. "Do you understand me, Mathieu? I don't care what happens, and I don't care who hurts you. I will be here to protect you. I promise."

"I know Momma," he cried, "but I just miss Dad. I really miss him."

"I know, Baby. I miss him too."

My son and I cried together until he fell asleep. We talked, and we cried. I suppose I should be happy that we can communicate like we do, but it really doesn't make it any easier that I don't have all the answers to communicate with.

I suppose that's a part of healing, as well – to be able to accept the things you can not change.

I told Jacob I thought it was best for him to let me and the boys spend time alone without him coming by because I didn't want them to get the impression that he was coming back home if they saw him there. Over the next couple of days I received at least two or three calls a day from him. Each call came with a different excuse. Of course, his first was that he had just called to check on the boys. He wanted to be sure that Jackson was recovering okay and that his post-op doctor's visit had gone well. Then he called to ask if I had taken care of the house deed. One day he finally broke. The boys were at school, so I was at home alone. Jacob called just to see how I was doing. I must admit that a part of me felt good to have him show some sort of concern about my well-being. However, I had meant every word I said about not becoming the other woman. I was very short with him, but assured him that I was fine. I told him that I felt it was inappropriate for him to call me about anything other than child support or visitation. I sealed the deal by suggesting that he call my lawyer if he had any further concerns. I believe that second only to my conversation with Mathieu, that conversation was the hardest thing I've ever had to do in my life. I knew that if I was ever going to heal I needed time away from him. I was determined not to let him interfere with that process just because we happened to have a child together.

I spent a lot of time out of the house after that. I went shopping with my mother for my trip to Puerto Rico. Jada and I made lunch a daily affair. During the evening hours, I took the boys to see a few movies. I was determined to do anything to get me away from that house and, more importantly, my phone. I even went to see my office. It was great being in the building without having to work. I made mental plans for how I would decorate my office. Then I went shopping for work clothes. I don't believe I really needed any new clothes, but I was determined to make use of the extra money I was going to have thanks to my raise and the fact that the house was now paid off. After about a week, I had this out and about thing down. All I had left to do was pack for Puerto Rico.

Epilogue
The Rebirth

It had been a week and a half since I had last seen
Jacob. We had talked on the phone about Jackson and
Mathieu, but I was determined not to see him face to face
again until I was absolutely ready. I even had my mother
come by when I knew he would be picking up the boys. I
went out to get a few things for the house while she waited
for Jacob. She said he asked about me when he got there,
but I'm sure he was too embarrassed to inquire too much.
Lena had agreed to keep Jackson and Mathieu while I was
in Puerto Rico. I knew Jacob would want to see the boys
while I was out of town, so I called him to make sure he
had Lena's number. Jacob's mother cut that conversation
short. I was sure she was eavesdropping, but she claimed
she had picked up the telephone in the other room and
didn't know that anyone was on the line. It didn't matter
to me what her reason was. I was just all too happy not to

have to deal with her drama anymore. This was the day I was scheduled to leave, and I wasn't going to let anyone ruin it.

I was a bundle of nerves as I prepared to board the flight. There was nothing unusual about the trip itself. I was used to meeting clients all over the globe. The difference was that this time I was the leader of this team. I knew I had the best staff working with me. (Paula alone would have been enough.) I still couldn't help feeling like a child on the first day of school. This was a wonderful opportunity for me, and I didn't want to mess it up. I kept reciting all the things I knew about this company over and over again in my head. I began to bounce numbers around from our productivity reports on ads for other resorts. Just then I heard them call for us to board.

I got on the plane and took my seat. Paula sat down right next to me.

"Nervous, Ms. Peterson?"

"Never!" I gave her a fake smile.

"Me, too" she said. "It's just good to know they're sending me with the best."

"I feel the same way, Paula." I smiled.

The flight was much shorter than I expected. Maybe it was just my nerves. I had a drink when we left the airport and I believe I slept most of the way after that. I woke up to find myself above one of the most beautiful landscapes I've probably ever seen. I thought to myself how wonderful it would be to bring the boys with me the next time. I decided we would plan a summer trip as soon as I got back home.

Looking out that window, I felt like I was where I belonged. It was like this job was what I was born to do, and I knew it. All the fears I had about this project immediately disappeared right there in mid-air. I was thinking about other things now. Was I going to let Jackson go to the private pre-school Lena had been raving about? What color did I want to paint my kitchen? Did Mathieu really have to play football next year if he didn't want to? I saw no reason why he couldn't pick another sport next year. Maybe he wanted to stop playing sports altogether. He and I had been talking about the subject at different intervals. I felt like he was just going through a transitional phase at first, but maybe he really just didn't like it. I would make an effort to listen to him more carefully when we revisited the issue. I was so proud of the stronger bond we had now.

The best thing about asking myself all those questions was that I was the one with the answers. ME! I didn't have to wait for joint approval or for someone to tell me my ideas were okay. It was like I was being reborn. I realized that being single was not a sentencing, but rather a sort of graduation for me. I had been putting other peoples desires before my own for years. Now I only had to think about myself and my children. This was wonderful! I sat back in my seat rather satisfied with myself. I guess I must've stretched my legs out too far, because I kicked over my briefcase. I thought I had secured the locks, but apparently I hadn't because the case flew open. There lying on the floor beside it was one lone business card.

The G.Q. Spot

Owner and Operator - Gerald Quintin Adams

Once again, my mind revisited the list of things to do once I got back home. I saved the number to my cell and mentally penciled in one more phone call I would have to make. Yes, I thought to myself as I carefully tucked the card away in my purse, this single thing is really going to be fun!

Special Thanks

To God who saw fit to put writing in my soul. It is my goal to put You first in all I do. Even when I fail, You still keep loving me. How awesome is that!

This has been a long road, and I owe thanks to a lot of people for all their support in helping me make this dream a reality. There are a few in particular that I would like to name: Mary Dougherty – Editorial Assistance; Nedra Gammage – Editorial Assistance; Nastassia Rucker – Reader's perspective; Bernard Simon of KoolmintKreative – Cover art. Thanks to anyone who read my preview and decided to buy my book. You all make it possible, and I hope to bring you much more to read in the future!

j.b.

Character Names And
Their Meanings

Jacob – liar

Kumani – lioness

Salihah – right or correct

Nilaja (Naji) – pretty

I found all of these names on various websites. I just thought they would be interesting to weave into the story.

Book Club Discussion Questions

Do you think Jacob really loved Shamonica? Why? Why not?

Do you feel that he had a real choice in whether or not to marry Salihah?

Was Shamonica wrong to sleep with Jacob even after he was married? Explain.

Was Naji wrong to "rat out" her brother when Shamonica came to see her?

What do you think of Kumani? Does she really have her son's best interest at heart?

Very little was said about Salihah. What do you think of her? Did she trap Jacob?

What would you like to ask the author about *The Eighth Day* if you had an opportunity to meet her?

Printed in the United States
126531LV00001B/103-210/P